THE WHITE BATHING HUT

THORVALD STEEN

The White Bathing Hut

TRANSLATED BY
JAMES ANDERSON

LONDON NEW YORK CALCUTTA

Seagull Books, 2021

First published in Norwegian as *Det hvite badehuset* by Thorvald Steen
© Forlaget Oktober AS, Oslo, 2017
Published in agreement with Oslo Literary Agency

First published in English by Seagull Books, 2021
English translation © James Anderson, 2021

This translation has been published with the financial
support of NORLA

ISBN   978 0 8574 2 884 4

Typeset by Seagull Books, Calcutta, India
Printed and bound by Versa Press, East Peoria, Illinois, USA

THE WHITE BATHING HUT

A voice on the radio tells me that the Northern Lights will be visible from parts of eastern Norway tonight. I've never seen the Northern Lights before, but they say they're like green flames licking across the night sky. I check Wikipedia on my mobile phone. In the olden days, our forefathers regarded the Northern Lights as harbingers of famine and plague. I put the phone back in the inside pocket of my blue knitted jacket.

With one hand, I draw the curtain aside. I work the wheelchair forward to take a look out of the living-room window. The sky is black. Not a single star in sight. Most people on the planet have never seen the Northern Lights and they seem to manage perfectly well.

During the past year, I've become increasingly dependent on a wheelchair. I've come to accept it; the wheelchair can at least compensate for the helpless condition of my legs. A year ago I was falling so frequently that my wife, Sunniva, was worried I'd start breaking bones. It's happened before. If I fall, I can't get up without help. It's hard to admit that the muscle-wasting disease has reached a stage where a wheelchair is the only safe option.

I hunt in my bookshelves for an English biography of Napoleon Bonaparte. Could I have lent it to someone?

My mobile rings.

I thought it was in silent mode. I try to switch it off, fumble, then let the call through.

'Who is it?' I enquire tetchily.

'I've been trying to get hold of your mother,' says a woman's voice. 'She's not answering. Is there something the matter with her?'

'I think you've got the wrong number,' I say, about to cut her off.

'Would you tell your mother that one of her relations is dead?'

She comes out with a name that doesn't mean anything to me.

'My condolences,' I say, without really understanding the connection.

'He was well over ninety.'

'It's sad all the same,' I say.

'Well, that's what happens, losing someone is never easy.'

'But who are you?' I ask.

There's a pause before she answers:

'Eline.'

'Should I know the deceased?' I enquire.

I try to conjure up my relatives: my mother, with her curls that once were tinged with red, her cheekbones, her firm chin and slender nose is the easiest to imagine, but also my father's black, swept-back hair with its centre parting and his narrow, gentle eyes are reasonably clear in my mind, even though he's been dead a good while. I have some memories of my grandmother, despite the passage of more than forty years. Grandma had pale skin, greenish-brown eyes, smoked Pall Mall cigarettes incessantly and was mad about Solitaire. The cards were yellow with nicotine. She didn't say much but listened all the better for that, and she never corrected me. My father's parents died before I was born. His sister moved to Australia when I was four. My father's family could be linked to a photograph, a story, a trade and an address. All my mother's relations, apart from Grandma and one of her sisters, Ine, whom I'd met just once, were and remain invisible to me.

I've never known the name of my maternal grandfather. My mother's always refused to divulge it. All my life she's given the impression that she hasn't had any contact with the families of either of her parents. Whenever I asked why, she'd go quiet or become cross because she didn't want the subject raised. At a time when so many people are interested in their family trees, I, in my sixtieth year, have had to come to terms with the fact that I know nothing.

'Don't worry about your mother,' Eline continues. 'I'll write to her about her uncle.'

'I'm sorry,' I say. 'Perhaps I'm being a bit slow, but why are you phoning me? How did you get hold of this number?'

'I'm your cousin.'

'That can't be right. I haven't got one.'

'Yes, you have,' she says, her tone self-possessed. '*I'm* your cousin,' she repeats. 'I know who you are. Finding your number wasn't difficult.'

'Hang on a moment, I must just take a saucepan off the stove,' I interject to give myself time to think.

This isn't a dream. I'm awake. I notice that Chet Baker's 'Let's Get Lost' is playing on the radio. I lay the mobile in my lap and pull the knitted jacket closer about me. It's cold, and in a few days' time it'll be Advent. When I was a boy I used to look forward to Christmas Eve at this time of year, now I'm waiting for spring and the blackbird's song.

I lift the phone to my ear.

Eline's voice is mild and friendly. She's five years older than me and was twelve when she'd seen me for the first time. She was walking down Bogstadveien with her father. She spotted her grandmother on the opposite pavement with a fair-haired boy in a red-and-black tartan shirt and dark shorts. Eline, who was supporting her father, called out to her grandmother. Her grandmother just carried on, walking a little faster. Eline called out again. The only person who looked round was me, the unfamiliar boy, and I soon turned my gaze to the front once more. Eline's father shook her arm and told her to stop shouting. Once her grandmother and the boy had disappeared from view, she asked her father who the boy was. At first he wasn't forthcoming. Eline threatened to let go of him. It was only when she promised not to tell anyone that her father revealed that the boy was her seven-year-old cousin.

Eline had asked why she hadn't been allowed to talk to me. Her father hesitated, then said that the boy's parents didn't want anything to do with them.

I heard Eline draw breath. I was about to ask if we'd passed each other on other occasions.

'You realize that my father suffered from the same condition as you?' she said.

'What?' I said.

I tried to frame a question about the origin and development of her father's illness. But it eluded me.

Eline described how, after the incident in Bogstadveien, she'd made her way to her grandmother's in Sporveisgata on several occasions after school and hidden behind a skip that stood near the entrance to her flat. There she'd waited for me. Eline had surmised that as she fetched her grandmother's groceries for half the week, I might be the one who did it the other half.

I visited our mutual grandmother every Tuesday after school, and the shopping list was almost always the same: three packets of Pall Mall, bread, ham, cheese and coffee. Eline reckoned she'd bought roughly the same things. Sometimes at night, before Eline went off to sleep, she'd make up conversations between us:

'Let's do Grandma's shopping together one day, shall we?'

'Maybe we should take Grandma with us to the European Skating Championships at Bislett this weekend so that she can see Per Ivar Moe and Knut Johannesen properly?'

'Will you play chess with me?'

When Eline was confirmed, Grandma went to Lambertseter Church and to the dinner afterwards. Once Grandma and the other guests had gone, Eline was left sitting with her parents. She was pleased with the party, except for one thing: her young cousin hadn't been there. During dinner she'd mentioned the same thing to her grandmother, who'd suggested to Eline that she had a word with her father.

'But why wasn't I invited?' I asked impatiently.

Her father had explained that my mother thought being a house painter wasn't good enough. Later on, when his illness prevented him from doing such heavy work, he got an office job. He could speak some English and could write well. His name was Frode and he was four years older than my mother.

I told Eline that I'd served an apprenticeship as a painter and decorator too, and had worked in the trade for years until I was forced to take up teaching because of ill health.

Like me, Eline's father was very keen on chess. Frode had seen me sitting a couple of tables away during a tournament in St Olavsgate when I was fifteen.

During our conversation it struck me that I hadn't seen my uncle and my cousin at Grandma's funeral. I've attended various interments and seen the way families can lay aside their differences for the duration of the ceremony. It seems that death can prick the conscience and turn hard-heartedness into something akin to forgiveness.

Apart from our small nuclear family, only five others were present in the chapel. They were friends of Grandma's.

Eline recounted how she and her father had seen the obituary in the *Aftenposten* a fortnight after Grandma died. *It was a quiet funeral in accordance with the wishes of the deceased*, it said. The look of anguish on her father's face had stopped her from mentioning her grandmother's death ever again.

Eline said that her father knew—how she didn't under-stand—that I'd inherited his disease. According to her, I resem-bled both her father and the grandfather we shared, whose photo she'd kept. The mouth and the facial lopsidedness were the same. My grandfather's name was Tor.

Grandma always came to us for Sunday lunch, as well as Christmas and Easter. She saw in the New Year with 'the girls'—her friends. Eline said that Grandma rarely if ever went to their home in Radarveien, except during the three years my parents and I lived abroad. My father taught in Ethiopia in the 1950s, at the technical college in Addis Ababa.

On the rare occasions Grandma did visit Eline's family, she'd take the Metro to Lambertseter station, settle herself in the wing chair in the living room, get out her packet of Pall Mall and smoke incessantly, except when raising a coffee cup to her lips. Grandma always asked Eline how she was and what she'd been doing since they last met. Occasionally, Grandma would talk about herself. At such times, she'd almost invariably speak about her trip to America when she visited her sister Ine and Ine's husband in the Bronx district of New York. Eline never tired of hearing about the skyscrap-ers, the huge, fancy American cars that rolled through the streets, and the various precincts with their different popula-tions and nationalities. Grandma carried a brown envelope full of colour photographs from the trip in her handbag.

'Hey, so you saw them too?' I exclaimed.

'Yes,' she said laughing.

Then I started laughing too, as if this were a perfectly normal conversation between two cousins.

I could hear Eline's voice in my ear. I thought of my mother who would never talk about her father. Whenever I broached the subject, she said that I was never to ask again because it was too painful. She wouldn't reveal his name, where he came from or where he lived. He married Grandma in 1919. My mother was born in 1925. She said that her father sanded parquet flooring and drank and, because of his drinking, Grandma had left him after ten years of marriage. Throughout my youth and for most of my adult life I've felt that that was a brave decision for a woman in the 1930s. Later on, Grandma got married again, to a man on the west side of town who died of a thrombosis three years later.

I listen to Eline's voice and imagine her as the child standing behind that skip and glimpsing me as I slipped into Grandma's entrance. She'd viewed me over the years through one-way glass, the sort the police and psychiatrists use for observing suspects or patients.

Eline chatted on about her mother and father. I was silent, I heard only snippets of what she said. I was drained and numb. My head was an empty hangar and every plane and bird and insect was flying around above me.

'Good night,' was the last thing I said.

'Happy Advent,' Eline replied.

Smoke and exhaust fumes rise from the cars outside.

Their rear lights are a red river of lava running slowly down towards the black fjord and the cauldron of the city, its shards of light showering the window pane and my own watching eyes.

The calendar on the wall says it's the 17th of December. I have spent the morning, afternoon and evening writing out as accurately as I can, every exchange between my mother and myself during my two Advent visits. I thought that committing them to paper would induce a kind of detachment, and maybe even some tranquillity. I say the lines, mull them over and think.

I've left my phone and my personal alarm on top of the bookshelf, together with a sheet of paper bearing the words: *Same sky, different horizon.* This title is as far as I've got with an article I've promised the Features Desk of *Dagsavisen.* I'm to write about how attitudes towards Napoleon Bonaparte vary according to the part of the world you find yourself in. It irks me that I can't get started. As a freelance, I need all the commissions I can get. I began writing articles about historical figures when teaching got too demanding.

When we said goodbye this morning, I promised Sunniva I'd wear my alarm on my wrist and keep my phone on me so that I could summon help if I fell. Extra care is needed as my personal carer is on holiday until after Christmas and our daughter, Karoline, is spending a long weekend in Berlin with her boyfriend. Sunniva reminded me that she'd have no mobile signal on Svalbard. In fact, she said it twice as she'd noticed that I was more than a little preoccupied after my visit to my mother.

In spite of all of this, I forgot.

I unfold the map of Norway. I lean across the writing table and examine the northern regions to pinpoint the places that Sunniva is visiting on Svalbard. She's travelling with a couple of glaciologists from Tromsø to find out how much the glaciers have melted during the past year.

I turn my chair to the right. For the past hour I've tried to put my mother out of my mind. I lift the map from the table to take a closer look at Edgeøya. The map is smooth. It slips from my grasp, I try to catch it with my right hand, I lurch forward as I remember the visit to my mother, the way she held the worn, red thermos, looked out at the birds and pretended not to hear. I stare at Longyearbyen and the islands that make up Svalbard. By far the largest is Spitsbergen, and the smaller ones are Nordaustlandet, Barentsøya, Kvitøya, Prins Karls Forland, Kongsøya, Bjørnøya, Svenskøya and Wilhelmøya, and a number of others so small they have no names.

I must have forgotten to apply the wheelchair's brakes, the footrests strike the floor, the large back wheels lift and the weight is transferred to the little wheels at the front. The cushion I sit on, rather high and hard, slips. My torso falls forward.

My head jerks forward, my chin tips down towards my chest.

My clothes follow me: a green shirt, black Levi's.

The garments cover my body, apart from my right cuff, which hasn't been buttoned.

A fluttering, green pennant at my wrist.

I see the wood-white floor coming up to meet me, and north-eastern Svalbard which fills most of the map lying on the parquet floor.

Like a tower I fall, head, hair, mouth, ears, jaw, forehead, hips, kneecaps, thigh- and calf-bone, ankles, toes, everything falls.

I see the brown window frame, the mouldings in the corner.

I can just make out the stand and the half-dome of the steel lamp a little way off.

The speed increases.

If I put my hand out, my wrist will break.

Snow sits lightly on the pine needles outside.

The flowering months are long past.

I continue to fall.

Blood is pumped thousands of kilometres through arteries, veins and capillaries.

Teeth are a part of the skull.

I gulp for air.

I don't raise my arms.

I don't protect myself.

My toes contract beneath the shoe leather.

All ten of them.

I fall towards the north.

The blue sofa is unaffected by the movement in the room.

The sun's ruddy rays are filtered through the curtains.

Light is streaming in through the window.

The curtain is slightly open.

The sun leaves impressions on the floor.

The snowflakes whirl around me in their slow downward journey.

My dust.

We only live a short time.

We know *something* of ourselves, not much.

Accompanying me, the handwritten pages float towards the parquet, with mother's words and my own.

The annual rings are lighter than the rest of the woodwork beneath me.

My heels are cocked, almost vertical, like commas.

The body is a star, a torso with five branches: two long legs, two shorter arms and a noggin of bone and cartilage, of flesh, skin and hair.

The head extends the torso's vertical axis.

The star falls.

The branches are lighter than the torso which draws the rest down with it.

I try to lift my hands to protect my head.

I move my fingers.

My centre, the body's centre of gravity, is just below my navel.

That elastic-walled balloon, the belly, embraces the bowels.

The stomach, intestines, kidneys, liver, spleen, lungs, lymph glands and pancreas are stowaways on the trip.

They obey gravity blindly.

The organs keep working steadily: excreting, absorbing, storing, filtering, consuming, cells are born and die.

The spinal column twists its thirty-four vertebrae, its intervertebral discs of cartilage with the soft, jelly-like substance in the centre.

The transverse processes and the intervertebral muscles facilitate torsion, they are the guy ropes that hold the mast of the back in place.

I fall with my legs under me, their long and once powerful muscles, fashioned for work and ski jumping.

The heavy thigh bones are attached to the pelvis by strong ligaments.

Ligaments prevent the knees from slipping out of joint.

The joints of the foot that once alternated between power and suppleness to hold the body erect.

What small, clever joints.

Energetic Sherpas, with twenty-six bones, comprising tarsals, metatarsals and phalanges, surrounded by ligaments, muscles, tendons, flesh and blood to drive the legs, the hips, the torso, the arms and the head upward and onward.

I land in a heap.

Soft and hard.

Textiles, hair, flesh and bones.

That's all there is.

What if mother had seen me.

The wheelchair falls after me.

The wheel strikes my right calf.

The wheelchair is undamaged.

One wheel spins.

The chair's cushion tumbles out.

All I wanted was to look more closely at the distance between Longyearbyen and the North Pole.

It's an ordinary atlas.

It's cheap; it's easy to buy, easy to lift, provided you retain your balance.

I attempt to reconstruct what happened before I fell:

I kept my left hand on the arm rest and stretched out my right arm, my upper body followed, I forgot about equilibrium.

I ought to have engaged the wheel-lock and concentrated on that one movement, bending forward without tipping.

The pages of manuscript are spread across the map and the floor.

I look up at my phone, lying there on the shelf, together with my personal alarm.

Sunniva won't be back for a week. Our daughter, Karoline, is having a long weekend with her boyfriend in Berlin, and my personal carer is on holiday.

I lie here, among my papers, watching my life passing before my eyes, and I run my rough tongue across the broken molar which will last far longer than I will.

I was fifteen and growing up. I took it for granted that my body would get stronger with each passing year and achieve greater and greater things. Nothing was more important than doing a long and faultless ski jump. My goal was to jump at Holmenkollen.

In December, just before the start of the 1971 skiing season, I was sent to the doctor after falling at the end of every jump during our first snow-training at Linderudkollen. My coach and I both felt frustrated. We thought it was muscle strain. To comfort me, my coach announced that it could happen to anyone, even the best.

A biopsy, a piece of muscle fibre from my thigh, showed that I was suffering from a chronic disease—progressive muscular dystrophy of the facioscapulohumeral type. It affects one in twenty thousand people and is found in all variants, from mild to aggressive. It's a muscle-wasting disease which gradually causes paralysis in the face, shoulders, upper arms, hips and legs. I would be risking serious injury on the jump-slope, the neurologist told me. He insisted that I give up ski jumping immediately.

'For ever?' I asked.

'For ever.' the neurologist said.

He'd sentenced me never to fly again. He assumed I'd be confined to a wheelchair within five years, and that I'd be bedridden by the age of thirty.

The doctor explained that it was a disease that both sexes can inherit. He made me promise to tell my parents about our conversation.

When my mother and father came back from work that day, they asked how things had gone at the doctor's. I replied that everything was fine and that I'd merely got muscle strain. A week later the neurologist phoned my father. Next day, at dinner, my mother said that I wasn't to tell anyone about my illness. My father didn't contradict her.

A couple of weeks later I laid a questionnaire on the table. It was from the school nurse asking if there was any chronic disease in our family. Mother ticked 'no' and said that if I told the truth about my condition they would use it against me, and us. 'The school will treat you differently to the others, treat you like a victim. Would you enjoy that?' she asked. Should a potential employer learn of the illness in the future, it would be an excuse not to employ me, she said. I read my father's silence as acquiescence. I nodded.

Four months later, I was confirmed. I didn't let any of the guests, ski-jumping friends or my coach into the secret.

The following summer I wanted to confide in Grandma. Whenever I visited her we'd talk about the old days. When she wasn't reminiscing about her trip to the USA, it would be

Edvard Munch's stately, stylish figure, the guests at the Grand Café, Fred Olsen's riches, the first trams in Oslo—or the duel between the speed skaters Oscar Mathiesen and Bobby McLean at Frogner Stadium in 1920, that would fill the conversation. She was delighted every time I asked her to describe the contest in which the American lost to the graceful Norwegian. When Mathiesen passed the finishing line, Grandma's hat had been torn from her head and thrown on to the ice during the cheering. The loss of her headgear hadn't troubled her at all. It was her joy at the victory she dwelt upon as she sat in her wing chair behind a cloud of cigarette smoke. *She* was the one I'd open my heart to. I told my mother that I'd speak to Grandma about my diagnosis. My mother asked me if I wanted to make Grandma unhappy.

Ine, Grandma's sister, was sitting opposite me. When the tram for Holmenkollen passed the Vinderen pastry shop, she pointed to it saying that the old brick building must be a copy of a larger version she'd seen at Beaver Creek, Colorado.

We were on our way to Frognerseter. But first, Ine and her husband Sean, Grandma, my parents and I were going to the restaurant. After that we'd walk to the Holmenkollen slope, and then take the splendid, teak-panelled tram back to the city centre. Ine stared at me as I peered out of the tram window. I turned quickly. Our eyes met. Ine explained how much she'd looked forward to meeting me. She and Sean had no children of their own.

My father commented on the view that was opening up: Oslofjord and Bunnfjord, and Nesoddland which divided the two fjords. My mother had heard his description of this panorama many times before. Sean used a hearing aid that was difficult to adjust, and enquired regularly and with unnecessary shrillness:

'How far is it to the ski-jump hill?'

'Soon, very soon,' my father replied, as it gradually dawned on him that this wasn't the moment for a lecture about the fjord's significance for Oslo's harbour and city.

Sean had never seen a ski slope before but he knew that Holmenkollen was the most important of them all. He'd used snowshoes and skis when he'd been part of the crew of the ship that had carried the polar explorer Richard E. Byrd and his twin-engine plane to Ny-Ålesund on Spitsbergen in April 1926. But ski jumping was something he couldn't understand.

Ine's skiing experience was limited to three or four trips to Fløyfjell before she was twelve. She and Sean had emigrated in the middle of the 1920s, from Bergen and Dublin respectively. They'd met at an Irish do on Thanksgiving Day in Brooklyn. The last time Ine visited her native country had been thirty-five years earlier. Sean had never been to Norway before.

Turning to Sean, Grandma explained that I'd jumped at Midtstubakke but that I was currently injured after a fall last winter.

We left the tram at Frognerseter station and continued downhill to the restaurant. We all had apple cake and cream, and a cocoa as well, then went on talking about the view.

When the others made to get up and start walking, Sean leant across the table and asked when I was going to jump at Holmenkollen.

'Excuse me,' I said and ran to the toilet.

I threw up the apple cake I'd eaten, then washed and dried myself for a long time. Fortunately, I had a piece of chewing gum in my pocket which masked the worst of the taste. They stood waiting for me by the exit.

'You were a long time,' my father said. 'You look very white.'

'I must have eaten something that didn't agree with me,' I muttered.

I was hoping Sean had forgotten his question. I avoided his eyes and collected my jacket which I'd draped over the back of my chair. After my fall we never spoke of illness at home.

When we were standing in front of the Holmenkollen slope, Sean pointed to the top and asked if that was where the jumpers pushed off from. I said it was. Sean gasped and stuffed his pipe full of tobacco. Shreds hung over the edge of the worn pipe bowl. He lit it with his lighter, a small fire burning beneath his nose.

What you've never known, no one can take away from you, he mumbled and continued: 'When will you start training again?'

'In two months,' I replied. 'I hope I will jump in Holmen-kollen in two or three years.'

I glanced at my mother and father.

The words came easily, even though they were English.

I lie on the floor and breathe unevenly.

I'm losing six hundred thousand particles of skin every hour.

I sneeze, the air from my lungs is forced out of my mouth at one hundred and sixty kilometres per hour.

I put my movements into words, even the ones I'm not master of.

My eyes close.

I squirm.

My knees hurt.

I breathe through my nose.

I try to breathe deeply.

My diaphragm tenses for a couple of seconds and then flattens for the same length of time, relaxes and assumes its relaxed domed shape, before tensing once more between the pit of my stomach and chest.

I take in air.

I hold my breath until I've counted to three, so that it's spread deep into my lungs.

I exhale through my mouth.

My stomach contracts.

Thanks, great diaphragm muscle, which gives me oxygen for my brain, so that I can continue to think and move.

I manage to turn on to my side.

I hold my breath and listen.

All is quiet.

FIRST SUNDAY IN ADVENT

Snow falls outside the taxi, creating a new city, flake by flake. An orange anorak on the pavement flares up like a flame before disappearing round a corner. The wind rises. Snow crystals turn into projectiles. Those who've ventured out bend forward as they walk to protect their faces and chests. The snow swirls up around car wheels like downy dust. It appears like a pale mist in one of the side streets. Further away the flakes fall heavier and thicker, so that the outlines of streets and buildings vanish into greyness. Suddenly there is a lull. The snow chases away to another town on the shores of Oslofjord.

The cold has laid its hand over us. The snow-clearing gangs push the snow into entrances and under parked cars.

I'm on my way to my mother's three-storey terraced house. It's not a practical living space for an elderly person, but my mother won't hear of moving to a flat that's easy to look after. She'll talk about the week's news, about sport, the weather and dogs, but not about moving. She's a 'home-lover', according to her.

'So here you are at last,' she says. 'Why have you come in a wheelchair?'

'I've done it to save energy,' I reply.

The last time I came, the taxi driver had to help me up from the bench.

Mother's gaze wanders to the bird feeder.

The driver pushes me over the threshold and places me by the kitchen table opposite my mother.

She's laid the table for us. Two bluish-white cups with Dutch windmill motifs. I recall them from my boyhood.

'I got held up a bit,' I say and hand over the red star of Bethlehem I've brought with me.

'Why did you want to come, anyway?' she asks.

'You remember, we arranged three weeks ago that I'd come along and help you with the Christmas preparations as usual?'

She turns her face to the window, her eyes rest on the Christmas sheaf for a long time, as if it surprises her that the ears of corn in their red ribbon have been fixed to the spruce tree.

There are few things I associate with Christmas more than the big Twelfth Night party my mother organizes every year. Throughout my childhood my grandmother was there, and my father's cousins and their families, as well as one of his uncles and his aunt. By the turn of the millennium most of them were dead, and only my mother and my close family were left. But the food, beer and aquavit were the same as in my childhood.

A starter of smoked salmon. The Christmas gammon for the main course with Brussels sprouts, red cabbage, potatoes, cowberry jam and gravy. Lemon mousse for pudding. After dinner, the grown-ups dressed in their best would settle in the chairs in the living room and drink coffee and brandy. The women often preferred liqueur. Three dishes had been placed on the table, two of them laden with Christmas cakes, marzipan balls decorated with walnuts, sweets, dates and figs, and one groaning fruit dish of clementines, oranges, red apples, bananas and black and green grapes.

We sang a song, the Swedish 'Helan og Halvan går', which my father had learnt in the student choral society in Trondheim. I can still smell the scent of the Christmas tree and see the tiny ornamental Father Christmases, over a hundred and fifty of them, the crib with Jesus in it, flanked by Joseph and the Virgin Mary and the Three Wise Men as well as three asses surrounded by cotton wool on top of the writing desk. Every year I wondered why the Virgin Mary stood there looking so sad, in her dark-blue cape, dotted with gold stars.

When I was in my second year at school, a Swedish couple and their daughter, Marie, were invited for Christmas. When Marie and I were shaking hands, I noticed that her movement was slightly clumsy. I glanced up. Her eyes were blue but her pupils were unnaturally large. She was blind.

I was fascinated by how deftly she managed her knife and fork, and brought the food to her mouth. After dinner we two children went to my bedroom and played with the tin soldiers my father had inherited from his grandfather. The soldiers were packed inside an old banana crate that was on the shelf behind the Christmas tree. I spread the soldiers out on the floor. Their uniforms were neatly painted. The best were the Prussians—fifteen black-clad soldiers with long bayonets fixed to the muzzles of their rifles.

Suddenly, without warning, Marie rose from her chair and took a couple of steps forward. The heels of her shoes managed to break five bayonets before I could stop her. From then on my father called her Marie Bayonet.

My mother brushes away a lock of hair that's fallen over her eye.

'Mother, I need to ask you something,' I begin. 'Why has there never been anyone else from your family at the big Christmas party, apart from Grandma?'

'You're so taken up with the old days!'

'Didn't Father want them there?'

She draws breath. I look at her pale face. A few years ago she began dyeing her hair brown.

'Can't you sit up?' she asks after studying me.

I try to obey the injunction, but immediately feel irritated because I'm doing what she says, without remonstrating and without thinking about the pain it causes my neck.

'The physiotherapist and neurologist say I'm pretty good considering . . .'

I sound like a truculent fourteen-year-old. Why do I have to explain myself to her, of all people?

'It's forty years since I was diagnosed,' I continue. 'It's only in the last couple of years I've had to use a wheelchair. I ought to use it more, to rest.'

'You're not that ill,' my mother says.

'I should have had my carer with me,' I retort.

'You managed perfectly well without a wheelchair before.'

'I'm getting worse, Mother.'

'Didn't you want to talk about the Christmas preparations?'

'I should be thankful that I've been reasonably active up till now.'

I'm trying not to raise my voice.

'You can get corsets that help you sit more upright so that your stomach doesn't stick out,' says my mother. 'They don't cost much, either.'

'A corset will make me stop using the muscles I've still got in my torso,' I say. 'I try to keep moving as much as possible. My appearance will have to take second place.'

'People look at you.'

'The older I've got and the more visible my disease, the more I've become reconciled to my body. It wasn't always like that.'

My mother turns towards the windowsill on her right and switches on the small red radio that Sunniva and I gave her. Frenzied techno-pop fills the kitchen. This isn't Mother's favourite station but she shows no sign of wanting to turn down the volume or switch it off.

'Enough of that!' I shout, leaning forward and turning it off.

She spoons coffee powder into her cup and adds hot water from the thermos.

'You want some coffee?' she enquires.

'No thanks.'

She pushes the coffee jar in my direction.

'Sure you don't want a drop? Perhaps you'd rather have real coffee?'

I shake my head.

'It's kind of you, but I don't need any coffee.'

She glances at the black-and-white portrait of my father which stands on the table in front of her. He's in his forties in the photo. The wrinkles on his forehead stand out. The picture was taken the same year I learnt to ski. This took place in the field in front of Huseby School. My father had put my name down for the skiing course. I was six and hadn't gone a metre on skis up to then. I had a lot of ground to make up. The course was run by the skiers company of the Royal Guards which had a camp close by. A soldier by the name of Per Oddvar was responsible for the fact that I learnt so quickly. While he showed me how to turn, Per Oddvar described how he'd been detailed to stand by the jump at Holmenkollen in full dress uniform and give a blast on his trumpet when a contestant was to start. How I admired him. If he'd told me to jump at Holmenkollen that evening, I'd have done it.

'Lately I've been thinking about something to do with Father,' I say.

My mother lifts her head and looks at me enquiringly. 'Are you going to bring . . . him into this now?'

'You remember our long skiing trips in Nordmarka? The longest would have been the one from Jaren and back home. We must have covered nearly fifty miles. Maybe Father thought the exercise would strengthen me so that I'd be tougher and better prepared when my muscles were weakened by disease?'

'I think that's fanciful,' my mother says. 'He always said that we were a skiing nation, and as such it was his duty to bring you up to be a decent skier. According to him, our greatest exploits had been achieved with skis on our feet, whether that was getting to the Poles or sabotaging the heavy-water plant at Vemork.'

'Perhaps he wanted us to do something together?' I say.

'You look older than last time.'

'Well,' I reply, mildly abashed, 'It has been three weeks since we last met.'

We normally meet once a month, a little more frequently at festive times of the year.

She bustles over to the kitchen sideboard and takes out the round, light-blue tin of teabags. She gives it a nod:

'Maybe you'll want a tea in a little while?'

Mother lives mainly in her kitchen where she can look out at the Christmas sheaf and the red-painted bird feeder where the odd great tit, and other tits whose names I don't know, come visiting.

I glance at my wristwatch, I've been here almost fifteen minutes without saying any of the things I meant to.

There's a radio on the kitchen table, a small television set, there are also books, scratch cards, bills, food, calendars, reminders—even last year's tax return. She's gathered together all the most important items. Those that aren't there have always been kept in the kitchen drawer. Photographs, letters and objects which, I suspect, she examines and talks to when she's alone. My assumption isn't unfounded. At various times during my childhood I caught her talking to herself in unguarded moments.

On the bench next to her are piles of newspapers and clippings. She's gone through Father's things and her own. I recognize two medals Father got when he was in the Royal Air Force during the war, and two of the rulers he used as an architect when designing bridges and houses.

'So you've been tidying up?' I say once she's sitting down.

My mother pours more water into her cup. Her hand trembles slightly. The sunlight brings out a gleam of golden yellow in her greenish-brown eyes.

'I've got cancer,' she announces suddenly.

I've been caught off guard.

'But . . . Mother, that's terrible . . . '

'There's nothing they can do,' she says. 'I don't want to talk about it.'

I don't know what to say. She shrugs.

Two other framed photographs stand on the kitchen table, in addition to the portrait of my father. One is a black-and-white photo of Mother, taken when she'd just finished high school in 1941. The other is a colour print from 1957. She's turning her face towards the camera, she's thirty-one, beautiful, in a houndstooth coat and permed hair, getting into a passenger plane. She's holding me by the hand. I'm two-and-a-half and wearing a blue cap and grey coat. Father must have been behind us taking the photograph. The twin-engined air-liner would take us to Hamburg. There we'd wait a couple of days for a plane to take us to Athens. Three weeks later we'd arrive in Addis Ababa.

I look at the picture, at her standing on the steps of the DC-3 at Fornebu Airport, a slightly more modern version of the plane in the farewell scene in *Casablanca*, when Humphrey Bogart and Ingrid Bergman say goodbye.

I've been dreading this visit, weighing up the pros and cons of telling my mother about the conversation with Eline. About her brother and father and everything she hasn't divulged.

Now she's begun to age, she no longer wishes to be pho-tographed. According to her, an immutable law decrees that elderly people are never lovely. I hold the empty cup in front of me, drop a teabag into it and fill it with water.

I wrap my hands around the hot china.

'Aren't you burning yourself?' she asks.

My eyes fall on the white frame of a slide in among the newspaper cuttings on the table. I pick it up.

'Stop,' she says, but I've already got hold of it.

I raise it towards the light from the ceiling lamp. She tries to snatch it out of my hands.

'That's mine!' she says.

I lean back to prevent her reaching it.

'Yes, it is yours,' I say.

The transparency shows Haile Selassie facing the camera and me with my back to it, bare-chested and wearing blue shorts. I see the slender back of a boy, with protruding shoulder blades. I also make out part of the back of my father's head on the right of the photograph.

One of my earliest memories is from Ethiopia: my toes are spread beneath me. All of a sudden I see how my feet look like two white crabs on a living rock. I have to keep my head up. I'm standing on a tortoise, the oldest one in Addis Ababa. The shell of the tortoise is greyish-brown, rough and worn. There are two small holes in it, caused by the teeth of a lion. Through the dust I can make out hundreds of people assembled on my right. They're waving, cheering and shouting. I hear drumming.

My hair is damp and dusty. My mouth is dry. It's boiling hot. I'm holding a wooden goad, wrapped in strands of yellow, red and green rubber—Ethiopia's colours. I'm five years old. I'm barefoot, it helps me balance.

The Emperor of Egypt, the god of the Rastafarians, is in front of me on the left. I keep my eyes on the emperor who's sitting on a throne outside the Technical College. His princes and princesses are seated beside him, three on one side, four on the other. I can count: one, two, three, and, *hulett*, *sost*, the way I learnt at the kindergarten where they speak Amharic.

Behind me I can hear shoes tramping in time on the sand. Ten students in every row, seven rows. Most of them are Ethiopians and Nubians, some are from Eritrea and Somalia, my father has told me. Father is their teacher, and I'm their mascot. The eldest student, Gebre, is leading the great tortoise on a rope. Close to the dais I can see a huge cage. It's been positioned behind the emperor's throne. The students have warned me so that I won't be frightened when I catch sight of the lions. They pace restlessly up and down behind the bars, one yawns and flicks its tail. I inhale and shift my feet a fraction.

Gebre is the tallest man I've ever seen. He's strong enough to choke a lion. Gebre leads me up to the emperor. We mount three steps to the wooden podium where the emperor is sitting. I fix my eyes on His Highness the whole time, just as Gebre has asked me to. The emperor's face is dark-brown, his cheekbones prominent, he doesn't look like Gebre. His body is thin. I glance for an instant at the bony hand which protrudes from a blue silk sleeve. His hair and beard are curly. I bow deeply. The emperor hands me a silver cup with his emblem on it. I bow even lower.

Afterwards Gebre gave me five stamps with the emperor's portrait on a background of yellow, red, green, blue and orange. Gebre told me that Haile Selassie was descended from King Solomon and the Queen of Sheba. I hadn't a clue who any of them were.

When my mother and father tucked me up that night, they smiled and said I'd been very good.

I was Ethiopia's proudest boy. The following year we came home to Norway.

'Give me the slide!' my mother insists.

I hesitate, but obey so that I won't be deflected from my real errand.

Firstly, my doctor has asked me to get the medical history of my mother's family, to see how things could be passed on. The genes dictate just how predisposed the next generations will be to contracting the disease. Secondly, I want to learn about my own history: Who am I, who were my forebears?

Could I have been a problem for her?

'It's three years since we went to the theatre together, Mother. I so enjoyed that. Didn't you enjoy it too?'

She was always the one who got the tickets and decided what we'd see. I used to drive her home afterwards. We'd laugh together and talk about how good the various performances were. Or we'd talk about uncomplicated things, Karoline, or memories of my mother's black cocker spaniel, Pelle, about next Christmas or next Independence Day. It was a way of maintaining contact between her and the rest of the family. For the past couple of years I hadn't been fit enough to drive my car, even though it's an automatic.

I notice that her eyes are moist.

'Can you pass me the scissors on the shelf behind you?' she asks.

'What do you want them for?'

'Must I tell you what I want a pair of scissors for?'

I place the scissors on the table.

'Should I phone your home help so that she can get your Christmas decorations out, Mother?'

'Certainly.'

We drink from our cups in silence. Outside the window, the tits fly back and forth to the sheaf. The sun is a hectic orange. It's just after midday.

'It's a good job you had it put up,' I say nodding towards the sheaf in the tree. 'The birds will need it. The weather forecasters say that December's to be cold.'

'*Had it put up?*'

'You had help, didn't you?'

'No.'

She shrugs. One of the tits begins to peck at the ribbon. We both look out. The heat from my cup reaches my chin. I wipe away the moisture.

'Is it because you were an only child that you're so self-reliant?'

'What are you driving at?' she demands. 'You're wondering about something.'

'Well, Mother, answer.'

'You know perfectly well that I was an only child.'

The day after my conversation with Eline, I rang the wife of a former teaching colleague. She worked at the National Archives. Might the secrecy surrounding my grandfather be because he'd been a criminal and had found himself on the wrong side of the law? I told my tale and asked if the records went right back to my grandfather's time. Could he have been fined for drunkenness, or were there other things on his record? She said she'd phone me back. As I waited, I wasn't sure in my heart of hearts what sort of answer I wanted. It struck me that if Tor had committed a serious offence, it would be an explanation of sorts. In a way, I wished it was that.

A couple of hours later she phoned back with the news that Tor had nothing on his record at all. Just as I was about to ring off, she mentioned that Grandfather's name appeared in the archives in connection with something else. Before I could say anything, she explained that Grandfather had helped launch two fundraising initiatives for needy tubercular patients. Tor had requested police permission and had been granted it.

I couldn't have been happier.

I'd never been to the National Theatre. Grandma, Mother and I were going to see *Journey to the Christmas Star*. Father drove us in the Opel Rekord. The roads were icy. They made my mother nervous. Grandma was as calm as ever.

I looked out of the window and thought of the forthcoming Winter Olympics at Innsbruck, where my ski-jumping heroes, Toralf Engan and Torgeir Brandtzæg, would have opportunities to win medals.

Outside the main entrance to the National Theatre, torches had been lit. Within the two heavy doors it was warm and full of children, some still wrapped their coats and some without them, and adults, mainly women.

We had seats in one of the back rows of the stalls. In the orchestra pit the musicians were tuning their instruments.

The purple curtain lifted. I sat there in grey trousers, white shirt, red tie and blue jacket. Mother and Grandma had their best dresses on.

A castle with towers and spires soared over a small village encircled by thick walls, right in front of me. In the castle lived the king, the queen and their beautiful daughter, Sonja. The royal couple loved their daughter. Around her neck she wore a golden heart her mother had given her.

Suddenly, on the very eve of Christmas, the princess set out to find the Christmas star, which she wanted more than anything. The count, who was dressed all in black, had tricked her into believing that it was possible to get hold of it. The king cursed the star, which was responsible for his daughter's disappearance. The king's words caused the star to dim. The queen, who was searching for the princess, lost her way in the darkness. The king was inconsolable.

Act One was over. When the lights in the auditorium came up my hands were still clasped to my face. The two women I was with were affected by what we'd seen, just like me. I told them I was certain that the count had taken the princess prisoner. I remember the way they exchanged knowing looks.

I'd been promised cocoa in the interval, but I asked if I could stay where I was, I didn't want anything. I said I wanted to think. They joined the noisy crowd which was making its way out of the doors. I looked around the auditorium which was emptying fast. I was sitting there inside something which, more than anything, resembled my idea of a castle. Around me I saw gold, rich reds and white.

Beside the orchestra pit an elderly, white-haired programme vendor in a suit was moving about. He was searching for something between the seats. I watched him surreptitiously, while I thought about how lovely Christmas had been and that autumn at school, too. The subjects and the teachers filled me with nothing but pleasure—no fear at all. I enjoyed learning. The round ivory box on the desk in my bedroom contained my first long-distance skiing certificate, my swimming badge and a coloured print I got the first time I attended Sunday School: an angel with pink cheeks, flowing curly hair and big blue eyes. His wings were only just visible and looked as if they were neatly folded between his shoulder blades.

At school I memorized hymn verses and gospel stories, with application and energy. The more I learnt, the better my results would be. That's what the teachers said. Effort brought its own reward. Always. There was justice in the world.

In Addis Ababa I was a child, now I'm almost a teenager I thought as I waited for the second act. I'd learnt Luther's Small Catechism, the Ten Commandments, and I said my prayers every day at bedtime. On the first Friday of every month, I put everything I'd earned as a florist's delivery boy into the school's saving account. Our class teacher called us alphabetically, and we went up to the desk and handed over the money we wished to save.

I was a precocious boy with a Protestant work ethic long before I knew the meaning of the words.

Each evening I said the evening prayer:

Dear Lord, I have everything I need,
thank you for all that I've received.
You are kind, you love me . . .

I used to end by asking God to help me become good enough as a ski jumper to take part in the Holmenkollen competition, to be clever at school and to make Frida Nilstun fall in love with me.

The earthquake in Skopje; the founding of the Organisation for African Unity at Addis Ababa hosted by Emperor Haile Selassie; and the world's first female cosmonaut, the Soviet Valentina Tereshkova, were events that I'd noted during the year. But it was none of these that concerned me as I sat beneath the National Theatre's impressive ceiling. What concerned me was the assassination of John F. Kennedy.

Imagine that a man, the president of the USA, who all the adults I knew spoke well of, should be shot and killed in his own country! Each day since the killing I'd imagined his despairing widow and broken-hearted children. Kennedy, like the king in the play, was a man no one could hate, I thought as I leant back and felt the soft, plush-covered backrest.

The day after the murder my best friend and I talked about how we could comfort the widow, Jacqueline Kennedy, and her children. We discussed which was the finest building in Oslo. I suggested Holmenkollen, but his argument that she'd be unlikely to know much about ski jumping, was decisive and so we opted for the *biggest* building we knew of in our city. Accordingly, we immediately set to work making a 1 x 0.75–metre polystyrene model of Akershus Fortress and Palace. We spent two weeks modelling it with Stanley knives before painting it in excruciating detail and naturalistic colours. We used the same paints we finished our model planes with.

Father came with us to the main post office in Tollbodgate. We sent the model to Jacqueline Kennedy so that she'd have something else to think about. It was a large parcel, but mercifully not very heavy. The post-office clerk at the counter initially said it would have to go by sea, but when my father explained the idea behind it and the man opened the window and caught sight of me, he stamped the parcel with a large Air Mail frank.

The fact that we'd managed to send it off to the White House, 1600 Pennsylvania Avenue, Washington, District of Columbia, United States of America, in good time for Christmas, filled me with relief, and yes, happiness, where I sat. Had the gift for Jacqueline Kennedy reached her personally?

A shrill ringing announced the start of Act Two, and Grandma and Mother and the rest of the smartly dressed audience returned to their places on the creaky folding seats.

In front of me were two lips. A mouth. It opened now and then. It was badly shaved beneath the nose. The nostrils were large. They flared. I glimpsed a pair of green eyes. I was staring at the large face of a man. A front tooth with a silver crown appeared. The tiny muscles around his eyes and mouth shifted constantly. A sweaty forelock of brown hair was plastered to his pale, furrowed brow. Were there sounds issuing from his mouth? Certainly, it was making noises. There was a pattern, a relation between them.

It was a language I understood, he was speaking Norwegian, the language I'd grown up with. 'Say something for God's sake. Are you alive?' was what he was saying.

He repeated the words. It was a little while before I realized that I could send some words back, for now that I thought about it, wasn't it me he was talking to?

I tried to turn my head to see if there was anyone behind me. There wasn't. I had the impression of a black wall with a rough surface.

I was lying on the pavement. I didn't know where. Several people stood around, I heard one remark what a shame it was that this should happen in Lille Grensen, Oslo's first pedestrian street. A place where people, in an upright posture, had passed one another in both directions for well over a century, on the way to and from the city's main street, Karl Johan, and the Norwegian parliament. Someone shouted for the police. I explained that I hadn't lain down on purpose.

I'd never fallen in public before. I'd fallen at home or alone but never in front of strangers.

Most had hurried past giving me a wide berth.

'Did anyone see him go down?' someone above me asked.

'He tottered, then he stood there swaying, and then he went straight down, as if the skeleton had been sucked out of his body,' said the man with the silver crown. 'I watched the Phillips building come down in Majorstua in 2000, not forward, not backwards, not sideways, just straight down. It was the same with him.'

'Is he drunk?' a woman's voice enquired.

'Don't know,' said another.

My head was raised. The man with the silver tooth put his head to my chest to listen. When he lowered his head, I caught sight of the sun. It was a cloudless day.

'Walk round!' someone shouted.

I glimpsed the outlines of several people grouped around me. Tall, short, fat, thin, they towered brazenly before my eyes.

They stared at me as if I didn't see them. And in a way I didn't, I saw myself, not the way I'd seen myself two dimensionally in a mirror, now I was three dimensional, someone who'd wrested space in society, a body in the way, a body I could study from outside.

An old man in a hat stood with arms folded. A younger man with a suitcase on wheels shouted. He was angry. At the very back, on the right, I saw an older woman with a stoop and greyish-brown hair. After a while I recognized her. As my mother met my gaze, my hands went up to my face.

Another elderly woman with a violet coat and white handbag nodded to her, said that they should set up a sign so that people could walk round.

There were just two of us in the green Volkswagen Beetle. I was in the back seat. Father was driving and smoking his pipe. We were to travel home to Norway in only a few months' time.

We found ourselves in an area we hadn't visited before. Father had to inspect some foundations one of his students had laid, and check if they were up to a professional standard. We drove away from the heat of Addis Ababa towards the mountains. Father said repeatedly that it seemed further than he'd thought. He told me to keep an eye out for anything resembling a petrol station, or more accurately, a pump. We passed one village after the other. A herd of zebras crossed the dusty road. Father stopped. When he tried to start gain, the engine wouldn't go. He banged the steering wheel, craned his head forward, tapped the petrol gauge and groaned. There was nobody to be seen anywhere. Father told me to sit still and got out of the car, opened the boot and found the petrol can. It was empty. He stood there a long time with the can, staring out across the barren mountainous landscape. 'Daddy, what will we do?' I asked. He turned to me and said that I was to sit in the car while he would walk back to the last village as fast as he could to buy petrol. I asked if I could go with him. He said that I'd have to look after the car, and that it would be quicker if he went alone. Wouldn't it be dark soon? I asked.

He showed me how to lock the Beetle from inside, before he sped off. The last thing I saw was that green can in his hand, before the cloud of dust hid him from view.

I quickly locked the two doors in the front and covered myself with the black-and-white woollen rug Grandma had given us.

I was awoken by someone tugging at the door. I felt a wave of relief. It was dusk outside. I sat up expecting to see my father. Both doors were being rattled and objects thrown on the roof. I saw shadows outside, forms that pushed and banged on the car. Someone was shaking the roof rack. I wailed, I pounded on the front seat and screamed that Father had to come. Suddenly, I heard a thud and caught sight of a couple of monkeys on the bonnet. They stared at me with wide eyes, their coats were grey and brown. Their noses flat. One of them let out a scream, I started and fell back. Straight away, the car was surrounded by dozens of them. After a few minutes the monkeys had managed to tear off the roof rack and throw it on the ground. Others searched for stones and sand which they hurled at the windows. The ones that weren't trying to destroy the car and get me, stared at me, cocked their heads to one side, rubbed their eyes, yawned, showed me their teeth and beat their breasts, babbling in their incomprehensible language.

I pressed my face hard into the back seat and cried. I heard something smash and saw a hole in the windscreen.

At last I heard men's voices. I raised my head cautiously. Three tall men with sticks were attacking the monkeys. They didn't run off straight away but attempted to take on one man at a time and snatch away his stick.

It was some time before the monkeys were forced to give in and disappear into the scrub and bushes, while my rescuers thumped their sticks on the ground and shouted after them.

Finally, I saw my father with his petrol can a little way off. When he came up to the men, he spoke to them and gave them money. Then he came over to the car, lifted the bonnet and poured the petrol in. I was still crying when he got into the car. He hugged me and dried my face with the rug. That night I dreamt, as I have so often since, of monkey faces from all angles. They glare at me, while I scream, unable to protect my face.

We sat around the dinner table. It was the second Sunday in February, I'd taken part in the G-12—the season's most important junior competition, also known as the Boys' Holmenkollen Meet. Father asked if I was happy with my jumps. Mother coughed and said she wanted a dog. Father looked bewildered. I glanced at them in surprise. In other families I'd heard it was children who asked for that sort of thing.

'A dog?' said my father. 'Have you any particular breed in mind?'

'Cocker spaniel,' my mother replied, 'a black one, I know where we can get it.'

Although I love dogs, I'd never have dared to ask for one. I thought the suggestion would be turned down because both my mother and father worked such long hours. Father's job, and Mother's as an archivist, meant that they often had to work into the evenings and at weekends.

Father's voice was mild when he enquired who would take the quadruped out for walks. Before I could utter a word, Mother replied that she would. A week later, Mother and

Father collected the puppy from Elverum. I was training at Solbergbakken that Sunday.

The previous owners told my mother that Pelle had a pedigree, a cocker spaniel of the finest breeding. He could win prizes at dog shows. Mother combed Pelle and clipped his nails regularly. He was entered for two dog shows. Mother was extremely proud of the fourth place he attained in the first one. Later I learnt from some other dog-owners that there's no such thing as fourth place. I told Mother. She said the judges were crooked. There were no more dog shows for Pelle.

Pelle loved being stroked and made a fuss of. He turned visibly jealous whenever anybody spoke to Mother. She was the one who usually gave him his food. Mother always said that he'd sit still and cock his head when she told him things. She stroked Pelle's back and scratched him behind the ears numerous times during the day, while she spoke lovingly to her 'naughty boy'.

When I was twenty and had already left home, I phoned my mother and asked if I could take Pelle on a hike. My hips were painful, but I was still able to ski. I picked up Pelle in my first car, an old Volvo Amazon I'd inherited from my father who'd died the year before.

Pelle bounded eagerly along the piste in front of me, with his long, red tongue hanging out. On the way home he disappeared into the forest several times, and I had to call out so that he could find me again. Quite suddenly, he collapsed in the ski tracks. He couldn't get up, his eyes were open wide, but he was breathing. A father hauling a sledge with a small boy on it stopped behind me. He patted me gently on the shoulder and laid Pelle next to the boy. Pelle breathed heavily, his eyes fixed on me, during the two miles back to the car park.

I drove to the vet's, phoned my mother and asked her if she wanted to come. She started crying and said she wanted 'to be at home with her grief'. The vet gave Pelle his final injection. Mother was off sick for three weeks. She wanted Pelle to be buried under the spruce tree outside the kitchen window. That was where he used to sit watching the pair of magpies which lived on the highest bough. I dug the hole for Pelle's remains, which were wrapped in plastic. Mother stood at my side. She wept bitterly as I laid them in it.

This is the tree she spends her time gazing at these days.

We were united in our admiration for Pelle. She always said that no one understood her as well as he did.

When Grandma died in Ullevål Hospital, I was the only person with her. I had a summer job as a nursing auxiliary. It was the summer before I was to start my third year at sixth-form college. Grandma had been a patient for more than three weeks and couldn't get out of bed unaided. She was clearly approaching the end. I was told to ring my mother. She didn't answer the phone. I phoned my father, who was certain that my mother was at home or was just out on an errand. She hadn't gone to work because Grandma had been so poorly the night before.

Only the two of us were in the room during that final hour Grandma was conscious and able to speak. I remember that I hugged the tiny figure in the wheeled bed. I held the thin, white arm with its visible blue veins. Suddenly she opened her large eyes. She stroked my cheek, smiled and said:

'Grandson, I'm learning the language of the other side. Soon you'll be able to let go of my hand because where I'm going now, I'm going alone.'

She breathed more calmly. Was that a good sign? After a while she began gasping for breath. Suddenly she was still.

Her face looked relaxed. I squeezed her hand, a little harder, and turned to look for the bell cord. I heard a sigh, turned towards her and pulled the cord. Her eyes were closed and her eyelids weren't moving. Before the door opened, I managed to register that her eyelashes weren't motionless.

I was still holding her.

Who was she really, this woman who knew about my disease but never talked to me about it?

Prior to Eline's phone call I'd imagined Grandma as that fragile, kindly lady who pushed my pram in Frogner Park. When I'd started kindergarten, she was active in the Norwegian Women's Public Health Association. She helped to organize Children's Day every year. For three years in a row I'd taken part, dressed up as a Dalmatian, in Father's cotton long johns, daubed with black spots. I'd stood on the back of a lorry with about twenty other kids and held out a long net to the public lining the route through central Oslo, to collect money for a worthy cause. Grandma taught me to make macaroon cake and to knit pot-holders, but these memories are like pictures that have been splashed with an acid that's eating its way in towards the centre of the motif.

I look up.

The ceiling isn't pure white.

It might be antique-white, but it's certainly not pearl-grey.

I assume that my eyes are still pale blue and my pupils are black.

It's possible that some blood vessels have ruptured and that the colour on parts of the cornea is red, like condensation trails at an air show.

There are pains in my head.

Could that be caused by my heart?

An iceberg floats within me.

I raise my head, I turn my face in various directions, I'm able to distinguish between walls and ceiling.

I say crow, mainly to get my voice to remind me that I exist.

Crow, I say again, I could have said anything to confirm my presence and assure myself that the words are coming out of my head and aren't remaining inside like packing around my thoughts.

I utter several words, they leave my tongue and fly out between my teeth and lips, they make up more than two sentences.

I fall silent.

Blood flows through my veins.

The veins surround the two hundred and six bones of my skeleton.

Today they're all intact.

I've forgotten to put my watch on.

I can hear water moving through the pipes in the walls.

Three dead flies throw shadows on the dust in the lamp bowl.

Dust is heavier than air.

It obeys the law of gravity, just as flies and I do, beneath the rectangular ceiling.

I've learnt to crawl, stand and walk.

A faulty chromosome caused me to lose that ability, but I'm still made up of living flesh, sinew, bone, some muscles, hair, beard, small bleeding ducts, pains, blood, secretions and nails.

I breathe between twelve to sixteen times a minute, it's a part of life.

I was born that way.

I've chosen to go on.

All my fingers are intact.

Both my long fingers are crooked.

They've been broken in two places and encompass their own symmetry.

I can articulate all my joints, not everyone can do that.

All the dust and flies in the bowl above me softens the lighting.

It's a pleasant light.

The outline of the things around me aren't too sharp.

This way you can sleep and doze when you want to, or study the objects in the room.

There are two closed doors between me and the front door.

FIRST SUNDAY IN ADVENT

Glancing out of Mother's kitchen window I say: 'Eline rang me recently.'

'Which Eline?'

I look at my mother. Is she really as surprised as she seems? I'm about to ask how many Elines she knows.

'My cousin. Eline. She's been trying to phone you for days. Why don't you answer the phone? It's not like you.'

'I must have been out.'

'She phoned to tell you that your brother's died.'

'He was old. It's no great surprise.'

'It was you Eline wanted to tell, not me.'

My mother is sitting a mere arm's length away from me. I look at her. Is she blinking a little more than usual?

'Why didn't you tell me that I've got a cousin?'

'Why didn't you put the phone down?' she says finally. 'It can be risky talking to people you don't know. The world is full of scammers.'

Her unpleasant remark doesn't surprise me. My mother has lived through a war. I haven't.

'My cousin's got parents. You had a brother.'

I search for a reaction in her face without finding one.

'I hadn't heard of them either,' I persist. 'That's more than just . . . unusual.'

She stares down into the half-full cup. Slowly she lifts her head and looks at me, as if she's about to speak.

She says nothing.

When I was twelve, I locked myself in the bathroom. I looked at myself in the mirror above the sink and tried to purse my lips as if I was whistling. I'd attempted it hundreds of times, without success. I tried once, twice, three times, four times until I had to use my fingers to push my lips into the correct position. The sound that emerged was nothing like a whistle.

'Remember what you said to me when I found I couldn't whistle, Mother?'

'I don't recall that I said anything.'

'You said that I mustn't tell Father. I didn't know why, but I didn't dare ask. You know perfectly well why I couldn't whistle.'

'Many children never learn to whistle.'

'And some of them lack the ability to learn.'

Her face reddens.

Is her cancer painful? Is she on medication? Doubt manifests itself. Is it too cruel to press her?

'Have you started chemo- or radiotherapy?'

'Don't nag.'

'It's a long time since I've seen you in that dress, Mother. It's pretty.'

This isn't untrue, but I hear that my words are, if not ill judged, at least a manifestation of not knowing what to say. My mother picks up on that sort of thing.

'You're clever with words, son.'

'Can *you* whistle, Mother?'

'You don't give up, do you? You're a strange one, to come home to your mother just before Christmas and go on about whether she can whistle or not.'

She clears her throat.

Even though I couldn't whistle I was still good at ski jumping and football. I made steady progress between the ages of twelve and fifteen.

'Do you remember how often I fell that winter I turned sixteen?' I say and continue, 'The first thing the doctor asked me was whether I could whistle. I didn't answer. I had the idea that a no would introduce something ominous, something threatening, like the shadow of a shark. D'you know what I mean?'

'I wasn't all that keen on your ski jumping. It's a dangerous sport.'

'I realize that, but that's not the reason you find the question unpleasant.'

'You seem to know everything.'

'Do you know why Dr Lachmann, the neurologist, examined me for so long and asked me to whistle? It's no good shaking your head. He said that I had poor muscle tone around my mouth.'

'That was a long time ago.'

'You want it forgotten or expunged?'

'You're so dramatic.'

'Wasn't it painful and difficult for you too? Couldn't you admit *that* at least?'

'There's no point in discussing it.'

'For me there's a point, Mother.'

'Not for me.'

'It's all in the past, is that what you think?'

'You're putting words in mouth.'

'I'm only doing that because you're not talking to me. I'm guessing. I'd like you and me to begin facing up to the things that have been hidden from me. I'm not expecting you to weep and wail, but couldn't you at least acknowledge that it's been . . . '

I search for words.

' . . . painful for both of us?'

I straighten my fingers, curl them again, turning my hand into a fist, I repeat the movement, become self-conscious when I discover what I'm doing and hide my hands under the table.

My coach and the school nurse, the companions I jumped with, and I myself were all convinced that my sudden falling was due to a perfectly normal sports' injury. We put it down to strain after the autumn's preliminary sessions of running and exercises for building up strength and suppleness.

'You knew it was more than a muscle strain when I began to fall, didn't you? Was there something about my movement or appearance that you recognized?'

'I can't imagine what you're driving at.'

I look at her. There is a silence. She doesn't avoid my gaze.

'The doctor said that I must never attempt a ski jump again.'

'There are more important things than ski jumping.'

'Not for me, not then. The doctor told me I'd become an invalid at an early age because the muscle-wasting disease would gradually cause paralysis in large parts of my legs and arms. He was honest, but luckily he wasn't right when he said that I'd end up in a wheelchair as a young man.'

Does she consider that I'm being sentimental? Does she believe I'm exaggerating, or is she suppressing everything? The fact that I'm unable to answer my own questions makes me realize just how little I know her.

'When Dr Lachmann explained what the diagnosis meant, I was shocked, I couldn't breathe,' I continue. 'I tried to get up, but I felt so faint that I had to sit down again.'

'You think I should have been there with you?' asks my mother. 'Well say it, then!'

Her face is very pale.

I could wish I was just as resolute. Have I inherited my parents' stoicism, so suited to the vicissitudes of war, but of little use in tackling my own problems?

'No, I was relieved that you and Father weren't there.'

'Why so?' she asks.

There is surprise in her voice.

'I didn't have to see the sorrow and disappointment in my parents' eyes.'

'Do you remember all the times you came from the other side of town to fetch Pelle because the black poodle was in season?' my mother asks. 'There wasn't a lot he was frightened of, but he caused many funny incidents, didn't he?'

'So you want to talk about Pelle?'

'Yes. Sorry, I've got to visit the loo.'

She gets up with difficulty and leaves the kitchen.

'I'll close the door to the passage so you won't be in a draught,' she says.

'Thanks, Mother.'

I listen to the shuffling feet. Her woollen slippers are a little too large. I lean forward and carefully open the drawer in the kitchen table.

The drawer is full of letters and old photographs, a few coloured prints, an old hair brush and a mirror that might have belonged to a doll. I listen for Mother again before taking out the top two letters. They are yellow and brittle at the edges. Both are addressed to Grandma. In two separate hands.

The first is dated 4th of December 1938. It's from Frode. He describes the daily routine aboard a large merchant vessel, the food, the waves, the gulls whenever they're near land and the people he meets in the dives of New York, Helsinki or Buenos Aires. He writes that he'll turn twenty in two days' time. He is grateful for the presents from his mother and sister, but doesn't say what they were. His tone is cordial. There is nothing to indicate conflict or animosity. He signs off *With love from Frode.*

I hear the loo door opening. I manage to put the sheets back in the drawer, close it, raise my cup to my lips and look out at the Christmas sheaf.

'I was rather a long time.'

'Don't worry about that, Mother.'

'Is your tea cold?'

'It's fine,' I say. 'I'm wondering if you found anything interesting when you sorted through Father's things?'

'That's a strange thing to bring up. I've gone through a number of photos and letters. Most of them uninteresting.'

'I don't understand that. Father was particular about throwing away clothes, photographs and papers he didn't need, so I don't see how that could be. It would be nice to be able to look through his things before they're . . . removed.'

'I've taken care of the most important things,' she says. 'Don't worry about that.'

'There's something you've never told me, Mother.'

I raise my head and study her face. She eyes me warily.

'I don't know what you mean.'

'Tell me about your brother,' I say.

'Who?'

'I know that his name was Frode. Now that I've found that out, couldn't you tell me a bit more about him?'

She stares at her cup.

'When Grandma was dying, I rang you up,' I say. 'Father said you were at home. Why didn't you come to the phone?'

No answer.

'Did you avoid taking the call because you knew that the doctors would ask if there were other relatives who ought to be contacted?'

She sits there opposite me, struggling. I think that's what she's doing. She's struggling for the very meaning of the life she's lived. Is she thinking in a way I simply can't comprehend? Maybe she has no words for it? Maybe concealment is a survival instinct? If she gave herself away, she'd lose her place and position regarding Father and me and the rest of the family? I can't make her out.

'Mother, what was it like growing up without your father during those years? Surely you thought about him and asked yourself how he was getting on? And even if Grandma didn't want to say anything, you must have formed your own ideas about why he wasn't living with you?'

Silence.

Our roles as mother and son are beginning to shrink.

There isn't much dialogue left.

I manage to roll over on to my stomach, slightly to the left, with my nose to the floor.

I can see out through the curtains, with their skirt-like pleats.

There's a small parting there.

Thanks to the architect who made the windows reach down to the floor.

Thanks to the curtains which couldn't be fully closed.

All the same.

There's not much light reaching my eyes and face.

It's better than nothing.

I can see more than shapes around me.

The chair legs, the wheelchair, the manuscript pages, parts of the map on which Longyearbyen and that infinite expanse of white, green and brown, which signify ice, mountain and plateau, stretching all the way up to Kvitøya and the Arctic Sea in the north-east.

I can touch the town of Barentsburg with my right index finger.

Carelessness is the cause of my lying here, in what for any species is a pitiful posture.

Now I can think about anything at all.

I haven't got to expend energy holding myself erect.

I can see my right hand, I make a fist of it and knock on the floor, once, twice, several times.

All I can hear is my fist against the oak floor. I knock once more and curse.

For dust thou art, and unto dust shalt thou return.

As for man, his days are as grass, I learnt.

If as an embryo I'd been able to choose whether to be a stone, a human being or grass, which would I have preferred?

Stone, scissors, paper.

One day all words will dissolve. The remains of letters, sounds—the *g*'s and the *z*'s.

I press my middle finger against the parquet.

My fingers crack.

Where will it all end?

At the mouth or the anus?

North, south or west, east?

I want to turn into mud, into earth, into dust, steam, molecules, atoms, into straw, leaves, bushes, trees, flowers, hill crests, blue spots in a cloudy sky, mountains, sunsets, seasons, raindrops, mist, sleet, snow, crystals and glaciers.

I shall be a part of this.

Karoline raises her arms straight out to the side. She twirls around and sings snatches of a nursery rhyme. Below her red T-shirt she's wearing a flouncy skirt of sunflower-yellow. Her legs and arms are brown. Her fingers stretch out. In half an hour the kindergarten's summer break will begin. She spins faster as she rises on the balls of her toes. Her toes spread out on the parquet. Insteps, heels, ankles and metatarsals spin above the floor. The muscles in her thighs and lower legs become visible.

She lowers her arms, her speed increases.

Her blonde hair forms a garland around her head. Her eyes are blue, her mouth open.

Suddenly she stops. Her heels come down, her hair falls into place. Karoline thrusts her arms out behind her and bows.

This is a story Mother has told me several times. In the third person:

She'd only just turned nineteen and was pushing a pram containing an eight-month-old boy. The baby wasn't hers. It belonged to a woman in Neuberggata. Since November the young woman, who would one day be my mother, had fetched the baby boy on the first Tuesday of the month at 10 p.m. She'd push the pram around to the rear of Frogner Stadium, the area furthest away from the lights of Kirkeveien. Having made sure she was unobserved, she'd extract a white bag from halfway down a litter bin on a grey-painted fence. If the bag wasn't there, her orders were to replace the lid and continue up Kirkeveien with the boy. She was to continue as far as Blindernveien, and then return to the flat in Neuberggata. When she delivered the boy she was to say: *The balloon has gone up*. That Tuesday, the bag and its documents were where they were supposed to be, under some newspapers, eggshells and candle stubs. It was important that the baby didn't wake. She rocked the pram gently to and fro, and managed to haul out the bag and place it beneath the mattress without disturbing the boy. It was cold enough for her to be able to see her own breath.

The year was 1944. It was January. The assignment was to push the pram up the length of Kirkeveien, past Middelthunsgate, Bjørnefontenen, onward past Majorstuen Church, Blindernveien, Ullevål Hospital, until she got all the way to Adamstuen and Geitmyrsveien.

Not far from the entrance to the Veterinary College was a metal drum containing animal excrement.

She was to throw the bag into it without being seen and push the pram back to Neuberggata, several kilometres away. Mother was in good physical shape. Before the war she'd taken part in several skating races. The five hundred metres was her best distance. She pushed the pram through the slush, away from the drum. Her footprints were obvious, and would probably become even more so when it froze overnight.

Oslo was a ghost city under the full moon. In three or four places she'd noticed chinks of light where curtains weren't properly drawn. She was relieved that she'd heard no aircraft engines, although she knew that the Allies seldom attacked when there was a full moon. They generally came when the sky was dark.

'*Achtung*!' Two soldiers stepped out of the darkness and came towards her. '*Achtung*!' She got the pram on to the pavement, smiled and said, '*Guten Abend*'. She showed them her papers which they studied carefully.

She spoke a passable schoolgirl German. They wanted to know why she was out so late. Where was her permit? Was this her child? She asked them which answers they wanted first. They looked at each other. She pulled out a permit explaining that she needed to walk the baby because of its severe colic pains, and that the child's mother couldn't do it because her leg was fractured. The declaration was in perfect German and signed by her doctor and the local hird commander, who the doctor supplied with morphine. The older of the two soldiers pulled out a torch and shone it on her and the document by turns. The younger asked her if she wanted a cigarette. She shook her head. The light shone on her face, moved down her green woollen coat to her fish-skin boots and up again.

'*Hübsch*!' said the older one. The other nodded. Still smiling she asked them to speak more softly so as not to wake the baby which had taken a long time to lull to sleep. In the light she could see that the older man was about her own age, the younger maybe seventeen and with pimples on his forehead.

'We'll have to search the pram,' the older one said just as a lorry with soldiers standing on the back drove past.

When they saw the young woman, they started whistling and catcalling. The baby woke up and began to wail.

'*Passieren, bitte*,' said the elder.

The woman crossed Suhmsgate and sang, 'Hush a bye, baby, on the treetop . . . '

I would so like to believe this story. I knew there were many female couriers and that there were Resistance people at the Veterinary College, but I haven't reviewed her tale in a critical light. I needed a story about her, a story just like this one. One that would make me feel proud of her. Did she feel that too?

I jumped into the water from the bathing jetty below Mosse-veien. Rolling over in the waves, I floated on my back without moving my limbs. I seem to remember the sun was peeping out. A little way off the red sail of a Colin Archer, smack cut in front of a regatta of all-white sails. I moved with the water and let my head and neck wallow and my arms and legs stretch out like a starfish. Sunniva swam on her back next to me, a little less pale, with her swelling stomach. She was preg-nant. The midwife had seen from the ultrasound that it was a girl with long legs. That was what we talked about before flicking water at each other and swimming calmly towards Hovedøya. It was summer, the water was blue. It was the last time I was fit enough to manage a bathing trip, wade ashore, feel the warm sand beneath my feet and bend down to pick up a starfish.

Father carried the rucksack. It contained an emergency aluminium ski tip, two sweaters, a spare pair of mittens for me, two modest packed lunches, a couple of oranges, a bar of chocolate and a thermos of tea. That was all. The rucksack was never to contain anything unnecessary. Not because of the weight, but because polar explorers such as Nansen and Johansen had taught Grandfather, Father and me that moderation, patience and resolve were prerequisites for enduring great stress.

The crack of dawn on Sunday morning saw us alighting at Grua station, a father and son, two citizens of Norway, the winter sports nation.

All winter we'd known it would be tough. A *gruelling slog* was the way Father described it. We'd been on similar skiing trips in previous years, when I'd been eleven and twelve. My father's description was accurate, but we were looking forward to it. The longest skiing trip of the year always took place at the end of March, when the skiing season was winding down. Nevertheless, our trips often had to be extended because of detours due to surface water or lack of snow. The main thing was to cover more ground than the year before. When I was twelve, we did thirty-three miles from the station at Stryken. Now we were taking the train to Grua. The trip would be forty miles over wet snow. From what Father said, the effect of spring on the sun-facing slopes had been such that brown grass and autumn leaves were showing through. I felt I was one of Norway's strongest thirteen-year-olds. It had been seven years since we'd returned from Ethiopia, and each year I'd trained with skis. These long hikes with my father were not just skiing joy and gruelling slog but also the one day in the year when it was just him and me. The day when we were completely alone together and could talk about our real interests without being disturbed by Mother. We talked about Nansen and Johansen and about Amundsen. We always discussed them and other skiing heroes. The kings of history, right up to Olav V. They all had a connection with the sport of skiing.

We didn't brag about what we were going to accomplish. We travelled on well-used wooden skis with rat-trap bindings. Just after the war, Father and a friend had skied from Trondheim to Oslo at this time of year. The trip had taken eleven days, cross-country. They spent the nights in barns and cabins they'd got permission to use. Just as he had then, Father got blisters. We had moleskin plaster that we'd cut into strips in the flap pocket of the rucksack, and these we applied to each other's heels. I felt something I took to be a blister before we reached Mylla, but I said nothing until we'd passed Spålen, Katnosa and Kikut. Father fixed the plaster and said that he'd got blisters just like mine.

We ate and drank what was in the rucksack.

We didn't visit the Kikut hut. The last bus from Sørkedalen would leave at seven minutes past six in the evening, and we had some way to go.

We'd had sunshine and slushy snow for most of the journey. Now the sun was going down. At the end of Lake Langlivann I could make out the shape of Nordmarka's highest mountain, Oppkuven. My feet and hands were cold. Father told me to take the lead and began talking about how the terrain from Langlivann down to Finnerud was often used as a hiding place by the best skiers of the Norwegian resistance during the final winter of the war. When I wanted to lie down because I was worn out, he told me about the Oswald group. These were the people who'd carried out missions in Oslo docks immediately after the Germans attacked Norway on the 9th of April 1940. By the time we got to Pipenhus I was completely exhausted. The weather was sharp and clear and my legs were numb.

'Feeling cold anywhere?' Father asked. I shook my head. My mittens, which I'd changed at Bjørnsjøen, had turned stiff with frost. He removed them, warmed my hands, massaged them and blew on them. I released my feet and tramped my boots in the ski track, hoping to get the feeling back in my toes. Father told me to keep doing it. I hummed 'Yesterday', to take my mind off the cold.

'Here,' Father said, 'I've got a surprise for you.'

I looked at him. From the breast pocket of his anorak he pulled out his half of the chocolate bar.

'This is for you.'

At first I wouldn't accept it. The chocolate was his, he might need it just as much as me.

'Son, I thought you'd read all about the relationship between Fridtjof Nansen and Hjalmar Johansen,' he said. 'More than once Johansen gave part of his food ration to Nansen, didn't you know that?'

I ate the whole thing in a twinkling, without saying a word.

We didn't make the bus, but tramped just over a mile along the Sørkesdal road with our skis on our shoulders. At last a car stopped and offered us a lift.

I've got a portrait of him on my desk. He was forty-two then. I took it with my first camera, the one I got from Grandma as a confirmation gift. When the photograph isn't in front of me, I notice that my mental picture of him fades. His face is in the process of leaving me. The crooked little smile in the left corner of his mouth, and the slanting furrow that I loved. The image gets more and more difficult to conjure up. Each time I look at his portrait, I'm reminded that Father never spoke to me of the secret and the thing that would become so important to me for the rest of my life.

'Dad! Come quickly!'

Karoline and I were alone at home. Sunniva had left for work that morning. I was sitting at my desk in the living room. My left hand gripped the armrest of the chair. With the help of my right hand I levered myself into a standing position after the left had grasped the bookshelf which is fixed to the wall. I placed my feet carefully in front of me, supporting myself on the wall so that I wouldn't go down.

'Hurry up! I'm in the bathroom.'

'I'm coming.'

Karoline was to start in the tenth year at school in a few months' time. I thought she'd cut herself and needed help. Some children do trip, cut and burn themselves more than others. Karoline was one of them.

She was standing in front of the mirror staring straight ahead, at herself.

Karoline's eyes and mine met in the reflection.

'Dad, I've got your illness.'

She wasn't asking, it was a statement.

'I've noticed it recently,' she said.

She explained that, as goalkeeper, it had become more difficult to reach high balls. Her right shoulder and arm couldn't move up fast enough to intercept balls or shoot out to cover the goal. More often than not, her left hand would push out hesitantly. She was in danger of losing her place as number one goalkeeper. She was ambitious. Her aim was to be the best in Norway.

'Dad,' she said, her eyes moving between her shoulders and my eyes in the mirror. 'Have you and Mum noticed it too?'

'Yes.'

She looked at me. Her look was full of wonder rather than reproach.

'For how long?'

'A year perhaps.'

'Why haven't you said anything?'

'For a long time we hoped it was nothing. We didn't want you to be unduly alarmed. You remember, we asked you a few years ago if you wanted to take a blood test that would provide the answer?'

'I didn't want to.'

She began to cry.

'I hoped that this would never happen,' she said, with a small pause between each word.

I can no longer remember my reply. I would like to have told her that life is so rich and varied that she might be able to learn from it, and perhaps, in the long run, become stronger as a result. I doubt if that's what I said.

I took two steps forward, put my arms around her slender body and asked:

'Are you OK?'

I really did say something as silly and helpless as that. I had never rehearsed my lines for this moment, which I knew would come. Sunniva and I had promised each other that we'd be honest and not hold out false hopes—but try to comfort.

'You've managed all right, Dad, in spite of everything,' Karoline said.

I was about to say that I was uneasy about her future and my own, but I decided to keep quiet.

I move my left knee up under me, it hurts.

I stretch out my right arm and push against the floor with my right ankle.

My left leg is almost straight.

At the fifth attempt I manage to get up on all fours.

It's a long time since I was last in this posture.

My mouth and nose are pointing straight down.

I'm surprised I've managed it.

I don't know how to celebrate.

I breathe heavily.

Time wends its invisible ways around me.

There's a thudding at my temples.

I tell myself that I must try to be calm and not flounder.

There's no blood on the floor.

I notice that my eye is sore.

Perhaps it's swollen?

If I try to feel, I'll fall.

I smell the dust around me.

I slip over on to my side.

I groan.

The ceiling is rectangular.

It isn't falling down.

It's supposed to be like this.

I'm torn from sleep like a page from a book.

Outside the window the moonlight lies gently, a gilded eyebrow on the blue-black cheek of night.

I must have fallen asleep while the thin stripes of sunset were showing.

Now the stars are big and glittering as if daubed with grease.

Beneath the stars, above the city, the light is parrot-feather green.

FIRST SUNDAY IN ADVENT

I look at my wristwatch, it's one thirty-five. It'll be an hour before the taxi driver comes to fetch me.

'A telephone call can change history, Mother. You've lied to me all my life.'

'Isn't everyone's life founded on a lie?' she replies and looks away.

Over the years I'd lived with the idea that the silence surrounding the family was due to some underlying event that couldn't be broached. In the end I gave up asking. That was good for domestic tranquillity but not much more, I thought, until Karoline was born.

'Why did Grandma leave your father?' I asked. 'Be honest.'

'How many times have you asked me that over the years?'

'Recent revelations mean that I need to ask some old questions again.'

'You know perfectly well that he was an alcoholic.'

'When Karoline's teacher told her to draw her family tree, Karoline couldn't understand why you wouldn't tell her the name of your father. And I—I defended you, Mother: *Don't nag you grandmother—she's got her reasons*, I said.'

What if she throws her coffee at me, or raises her hand to her heart and slumps forward, or simply begins to cry? If she does break down, is there a chance she'll say something? Would I continue to interrogate? I tell myself I would.

She fiddles with the handle of her cup.

'Do you want more tea?' she asks. 'No? I'll have a drop more coffee.'

And after a pause: 'How did you find Eline's number?'

'She phoned me, because she couldn't get in touch with you. Besides, Mother, Eline is pleasant and generous. She's got plenty of cause to be bitter. She wants to make contact with us.'

'I wouldn't know anything about that.'

Mother says this without looking up.

I try to keep the initiative: 'Eline knows the name of the grandfather we share. Your father. She's got pictures of him. She says he looks like me.'

'I can't take any more of this!'

'You've no need to get angry. You were only five or six when Grandma left him. You were too young to understand those relationships.'

I wait.

Mother picks up the diary on her left, and begins flicking through it as if she hasn't heard me.

'Did you miss your father after you left him?'

She straightens the sugar bowl.

'My father drank, and so we left.'

'Are you sure?'

Mother stirs her coffee. A little slops over the rim. She mops it with the paper napkin.

'Which of my symptoms did you recognize from your brother?'

'It's not a subject for conversation.'

'Eline and I have agreed to meet next week. Do you want to come too?'

Mother stares down into her saucer. Ought I to stop now, to leave her in peace?

'Do you want me to go home, Mother?'

In the first place it's impossible to get the taxi to come earlier, and in the second I haven't said all I wanted to say.

'Could you . . . '

She pauses a moment.

' . . . go to the living room and check that the Christmas lights are working? They're on the desk.'

From her tone one would imagine that we'd spoken of nothing but elves and angels.

'Eline's got parents. I had an aunt, whose name was Vivi by the way, and Uncle Frode, whom you've never let me meet. Your brother.'

'You're not going to help me with the Christmas lights, obviously. Don't you think it's about time I was released from this cross-examination?'

She rises and fetches a packet of Ritz biscuits from the cupboard.

I wheel myself over to the threshold of the living room. Turn the handle and nudge the door open, grip the push-rims of the wheelchair and heave as hard as I can to drive the wheels over the sill.

The box of lights is where the family portraits used to be. Only a black elephant from Ethiopia and a small silver pen-and-pencil case remain. I plug the lights in and screw in each of the bulbs until it comes on. I can hear her moving about the kitchen.

'D'you want the lights and the basket of little elves in with you?' I shout.

She makes no reply. I balance the basket on my lap and turn the wheelchair towards the kitchen. I shout again without receiving any response. Once at the kitchen door I push it gently open with my foot. She's sitting hunched over a sheet of paper with her glasses on, reading.

'Where do you want the basket?' I ask.

She pushes her glasses up on to her forehead and gazes at me as if she's surprised I'm there.

'Those, yes,' she says and points towards the sink. 'There.'

She lowers her glasses and peruses the text one final time.

'You can take a look at this.'

She pushes the sheet across the table, to the right of my plate, and says: 'Read.'

I register that the hand is unfamiliar. The date '1934' is visible at the top on the right. The day and the month have a blot on them. Grandma's name and address are at the top left. The ink is black, the paper yellow.

My dearest darling,

It will soon be night and I write to you to round off the day. Paper, fountain pen and memories after seventeen years. What more do you need to write a letter to someone you love . . . ? I can see you as if it were yesterday—that first time we met. My God, how young we were. Thinking back now, I can't comprehend it at all. Think of those times we shared at the white bathing hut. All I remember of that time was the sun and the high, blue sky. You come back into my life again, young and beautiful as you were then. Why can't we be young for ever? I know you still are. I loved you so much . . . Can you feel the shackles around my heart? You—you—you! You were mine and you are mine still. I love you.

Your own Tor

I clasp the thin paper and shiver.

'Something to eat?' my mother asks.

'Thanks for letting me see the letter. They obviously loved each other, even after . . . '

'Eat, now. I hadn't planned on letting you read it,' she says and goes over to check the contents of the basket.

It suddenly realize that I've got my phone in my inside pocket. I manage to take a photo of the letter before she seats herself again.

I must go on. I'm like a great rock, rolling towards a cliff.

I relate that Eline has told me all about how she, my own mother, and Grandma hid Eline and her family from me, and that Eline and her parents had talked several times about how I'd inherited the disease.

I need my mother to say something. I long for it. It's like a hunger to reach a softer core inside the hard shell.

She moves the dark-blue china butter dish.

'Eline was a child, Mother. Don't you think now, in retrospect, that you both behaved unreasonably towards her?'

'It was best that way.'

She still isn't looking at me.

'Why shouldn't I learn about my uncle and my cousin?'

'It's much too long a story.'

She begins spreading brie on the salty biscuit, takes a bite, looks up at the clock on the wall.

'Close your eyes,' she says smiling.

The uncertain expression on my face clearly satisfies her. I'm taken aback, but I obey.

I hear cups, saucers, knives and glasses being moved.

'Now you can open them.'

On the table before me is the pinball game. Seventy centimetres long and thirty wide. The game we always played on Twelfth Night.

The board is wooden. Most of the varnish has worn away. The twenty steel balls are about the size of marbles. The balls are struck with a red stick, a cue about eight inches long. Five holes and eleven zones are distributed across the board. Landing on them wins from five to a hundred and twenty-five points. The scores are painted on the board in blue. Each player plays all the balls and the points are tallied, and then it's the next player's turn.

'I thought we were only allowed to play pinball at Christmas?'

'I'm bequeathing this to you.'

'Thanks. I'd like that.'

'Let's play!' she says eagerly.

And she means it.

'Of course we'll play,' I say.

'You go first,' she says.

After four attempts I strike the remaining sixteen balls just hard enough, and my thoughts focus on the game. I manage an even push with the cue, which I used to be so good at as a child. After nine balls I'm no longer thinking about why I'm sitting in my mother's kitchen. My total is one thousand and seventy points. A good result.

'That was impressive,' she says. 'Now it's my go.'

She pulls the board and cue over to her side of the table.

I replace the balls in the magazine and she begins hitting them.

I look on, making occasional comments on the game, like: *Lovely, that was one hundred and twenty-five. Good shot, Mother. That's got to be a record.* I watch an old woman playing the tabletop game in front of me. I've become even more decrepit than she is. For several decades now I've managed to overcome the self-contempt of my teenaged years. Now, as I watch her play the balls on the board in front of her, the vulnerability and destructiveness I had in me back then, reassert themselves.

All her balls score points. Four of mine misfired.

'You've been practising,' I say.

'One thousand, four hundred and ten points,' she says.

'Congratulations!'

'D'you want your revenge?' she enquires.

'No,' I reply emphatically.

She takes the cue and holds it up in front of me.

'Can you see the marks halfway up? Do you know how they got there?'

I know perfectly well, but I shake my head.

'Pelle got so jealous when we played at those Christmas parties. You were the one who managed to pull the cue out of his mouth before it was ruined.'

She laughs.

The warm feeling from the game and the memory of Pelle causes me to blurt out:

'You had a difficult job during the war. You were brave, and you hadn't even turned twenty then. Was your brother a member of Quisling's NS? Did he help to torture Norwegians?'

'Have you gone mad? He wasn't a Nazi or a torturer.'

'So, did he do something else to you?'

'There was no assault, if that's what you're hinting at.'

'Then tell me the truth. Give me an explanation.' I hear the pleading note in my voice.

'There isn't much to tell. Silence is a human right,' says my mother.

'I'll have to go now, but I thought of visiting you again a fortnight on Sunday,' I say. 'Would that be all right?'

She shrugs her shoulders, hesitating, and then she nods.

I was convinced that nobody would ever love me. The secret I bore, that my body would turn me into an invalid, was one I shared with very few. I repeated the word in English. *Invalid*. It means *without value*. I wore roomy shirts and sweaters to conceal my increasingly prominent right shoulder, and my stomach which looked unnaturally large because of my deficient stomach muscles. I knew lots of people, but didn't allow either the men or the women to get close. I didn't want to be intimate with anyone. I couldn't see what good it would do me.

I stood thinking about all of this in front of the Tower Building at Gaustad, Norway's largest psychiatric hospital. It was Thursday. It was February. It was my twentieth birthday. I was humming Ramone's 'I Don't Care'.

I studied the red-brick wall of Ward A and wondered what mental patients looked like and how they behaved but also how I myself would be received. I'd heard that the hospital was looking for staff, but I didn't know what I was going to do with my life, or what I should train as. How could I make a plan of any kind? I didn't even know what I'd look like or be able to do in a few years' time. I hated my body. If anyone had told me that I ought to think positive, I'd have hit them. The weekends were the worst. Sometimes I lay in bed the whole of Saturday and Sunday without the energy to sit, eat or drink. In the mirror I could see that a few of the little muscles around my eyes and mouth had completely disappeared.

I stared at the frozen fountain in front of the entrance to the Tower Building. My hips and lower back hurt if I stood for long periods. When I walked, I could feel that my big thigh muscle had become weaker. I knew that most of the job applicants at the hospital were girls. One thing I was certain of: I had to do everything in my power to make sure I didn't fall in love. With real self-discipline, I could manage it. Maybe my self-contempt would help me succeed?

The previous year I'd lost my virginity to a woman who worked in a bank. I'd met her at a party. She was a friend of an auxiliary nurse I'd worked with at Ullevål Hospital the year before. She was nine years my senior. She said she wanted to get even with her husband, who for years had been carrying on with one of his employees, and I was desperate *to do it*. She said that my lopsided lips were strange but nice to kiss, and that flattered me. We made hectic love several times at her place while her husband was away on business. After that, if we happened to meet, we pretended not to see each other.

I'd become cynical and reckless about my life and safety. I'd charge down steep slopes on my bike without checking where they ended up. I'd walk straight across the road in the rush hour. I'd climb on to the roof of the Holmenkollen tram and lie there through the tunnels, all the way to Frognerseter.

The nursing officer said I could start straight away. When he asked if I was in good health, I replied: 'Of course.'

I was sent to Ward G, where the worst male cases were housed, according to the nursing officer. That afternoon I rented a bedsit on the second floor of the same building. Twenty-four nursing auxiliaries lived up there, the oldest of whom was twenty-three.

One Flew Over the Cuckoo's Nest starring Jack Nicholson had been released in 1975, the previous year. American hospitals of the 1960s formed the backdrop to the film. The reality on G1 East showed itself to be more brutal, unruly, warm and moving.

The men came from all strata of society. Most never had visitors. What they had in common was the diagnosis: *mentally ill*. They slept in dormitories, unable to lock up their personal possessions. The smell was far from nice, no matter how much cleaning we did. In addition, some of them were diagnosed as feebleminded as well as *mentally ill*. Most were given Nozinan to calm their worst outbursts. Three had been lobotomized fifteen years earlier. One had committed murder, and another had been castrated. A nurse handed out the drugs in the mornings, apart from the weekends, when a nursing auxiliary was responsible for the drugs' round. In addition to the nurse, who was often away sick, there was one nursing auxiliary and fourteen non-professionals.

One of the patients on the ward was in his mid-seventies. He'd been depressed for several months. His dose of Nozinan was constantly being increased. When I'd been there a fortnight, the consultant got hold of the male nursing auxiliary and went into the isolation ward with a metal suitcase. The nurse wasn't present. It was a Saturday. There were three of us on duty. The patient tried to hide under a bed in the dormitory. 'I've got a weak heart!' he shouted several times. I ran to the nursing station and looked at his notes. He was right. He was dragged, struggling, into the isolation ward. Several of the patients lay down and clamped their ears, a couple shouted at the consultant, some others tried to say something soothing, and the patients sitting in the imitation leather armchairs in the dayroom, turned away. A girl of my own age calmed the ones who were most distraught. The eldest patient, who had a big lobotomy scar on his forehead, led me to the small window in the isolation ward door.

'Look in there,' he said.

They succeeded in strapping the patient down after the nursing auxiliary sat on top of him. The consultant fixed the electrodes to his head. The head was bright red with two terrified, staring blue eyes. His white hair was damp with sweat. The consultant gave him an injection in his upper arm. The apparatus was on a bedside locker. Two wires connected the patient to the machine. It had a panel with switches, two dials and pointers. Through the small window I could see the auxiliary nurse remove the patient's false teeth and place them on the window sill, and then a rubber guard was put in his mouth. The consultant attached the electrodes to his temples. The current was switched on. The frail body convulsed. The blood rushed to his head and then he went completely white. I stood and watched. My arms hung limp. I saw the switch turned off.

The body lay still for a few seconds before it started thrashing about on the bed again, with its eyes rolled upward so that all I could see were the whites.

'You got to do something,' said the patient beside me.

He tugged at me and tramped the lino floor.

I tore open the heavy door with its scratched paint. There was a miniature screwdriver on my key ring. I ran in, shoved the screwdriver into the vacant plug socket and short-circuited the apparatus. The consultant shouted, I didn't hear what he said. I stood bolt upright, staring at the wall and panting. The youngest of the female auxiliaries, Sunniva, came rushing in.

The consultant ran to the nursing station and phoned the director to get me fired. The director didn't agree, he thought that would result in negative publicity for the hospital in the press. The consultant wouldn't speak to me again. The patient had lost consciousness. He was carried back to his bed in the dormitory.

Sunniva was a couple of years younger than me. She had a bedsit a bit further down the corridor on the second floor of Ward G. I'd spoken to her several times. I liked her, she had short hair, she was fit, cheerful and pretty.

That evening she knocked at the door of my bedsit. I offered her tea. She referred to the episode with the electro-convulsive machine. Sunniva said I was courageous. I shook my head.

'I was panicking.' I said, 'Doing nothing would have been even more painful for me.'

I sat on the narrow bed. She watched me from the spindle-backed chair on the far side of the small table. She had green eyes. We talked about *One Flew Over the Cuckoo's Nest*, the war in Vietnam and the mountains in the Rondane. When we'd finished our third cup of tea, she looked at me for a long time without speaking. Then she told me in a quiet voice that she was in love with me. I sat there with my arms dangling. She blushed. I must have blushed as well. I began to feel cold. I felt weak and numb. At last I replied that we could be friends but nothing more. I wasn't capable of returning love, I hadn't got the ability. I told her she was strong to dare to show love, and to express it. She thanked me for the compliment, but said it was little comfort. I said I'd lost the capacity several years before.

'What do you mean?' she asked.

'I don't know,' I replied.

'Good night,' Sunniva said and disappeared through the door without looking at me.

I went to bed feeling bad. I'd lied to her. I couldn't endure the thought of being honest and naked in front of her, my protruding shoulder blades, talking about the illness and how it would progress. I'd have to speak the truth and tell her that any children might inherit the disease. I couldn't have borne the shame of telling her that in the future I'd probably have to be nursed. I was a burden, a hindrance, an impediment, a strain, a complicated piece of living furniture.

I pulled the duvet over my head and hummed: 'I Don't Care'.

That first summer at Gaustad I got a job in the painting shop. I received the news on a hot August evening. A foolhardy notion took shape in my head. Five years before, preparing for the winter season, my coach had taught me an exercise I mastered well. The military dive.

My ski-jumping companions and I used to practise from the cliffs along Oslofjord, the ten-metre platform at the Frogner baths or the bridge above the Grini dam. That was almost fifteen metres high. To perform a military dive, you allowed yourself to fall forward with arms held tight to the sides of a body held completely straight. The head should strike the water first. During the dive you were supposed to look like 'a tin soldier who's not afraid of anything', as my ski-jumping coach said.

It was five years since I'd last done one, I'd been fifteen then. Early August was hot. Now, in shorts, T-shirt and trainers I stood on the railings of the bridge. It was higher than I remembered it.

My head hit the water first, then my lower legs and my body. I came to myself under the water. I scrambled up the stony bank.

I looked up at the bridge. Luckily, it looked as if nobody had seen me.

I'd taken on the task of painting the stairs in the Tower Building. The foreman thought we couldn't do the job because it was too dangerous. I insisted and got my own way. It was seven metres from the ceiling down to the steep stone staircase. We had no scaffolding or equipment suitable for painting such a high stairwell. In the store I found two four-and-a-half-metre wooden stepladders, and a set of planks which could be extended to ten metres, to stand on. The telescopic planks could rest on the top step of the two ladders, I explained to the foreman.

I stood on the planks painting with a roller that was attached to a long pole. A drop of paint in the eye or a false step while I was looking up, would have been fatal. I told the foreman that ski jumping had given me a good sense of balance, I wasn't afraid of heights, and I needed something to compensate for my loss of jumping on the big slopes.

What did I want to live for? I asked myself the question many times as I climbed the tall ladder. At the top, with my head turned towards the arched ceiling, the road to eternal darkness was a short one. I blamed nobody for my disease. I was suffering from something that went deeper. I was convinced that I lacked the gene necessary to accept love. The prerequisite ability to bond with another human being. I felt I had a pain in my gaze that I wouldn't find in anyone else. I wanted to beg for help but was unable to ask anyone for it.

I rollered on French Grey.

'Hey, do you want to kill yourself?' a woman's voice called.

I pretended not to hear. The words came again. I glanced down. Below me I saw a patient from the women's wing, Ward F, who was in her fifties and a patient at Gaustad for more than twenty years. She'd been to fetch the ward's post. She climbed three rungs of the ladder. I lowered the roller and met her eyes. They were clear and blue and stared at me from beneath a sou'wester. Her skin was shiny and she had high cheekbones. Sharp nose, gleaming eyes, as if she knew she was the only person on earth who'd discovered how I was feeling. I stared at her chin, it was trembling. I'd noticed the symptom in various people who'd used Nozinan for years. I nodded and continued painting. She didn't leave.

'Won't you answer?'

'I've got a job to do,' I said, not looking down.

It was the Friday before Whitsun. The next three days I lay in bed crying. That woman's perceptiveness made me think that maybe others could see into me. Her words made me ask myself: Who would care if I ended it all?

Many suicides are criticized for not leaving a note. I learnt then just how unreasonable the indictment was. There are no words.

I became a journeyman painter, and eventually foreman and the chief safety representative for the staff at the hospital.

This made it easier for me to talk about my illness to my friends and closest colleagues at work. The position was an expression of my workmates' confidence in me. Warily, my self-loathing loosened its grip.

But the management knew nothing. They could have got rid of me on the pretext that I wasn't fit to work as a painter.

I cycled from the paint shop at Gaustad Hospital to the University of Oslo at Blindern, a mile away. As I put my bike in the rack outside the tall brick building, I felt a sharp stab of pain and an aching in my hips. I tried to loosen them up but that didn't help. It was early September. The night had been cold. I was wearing my Icelandic sweater and paint-spattered trousers from work. Earlier in the day I'd phoned the Department of Philosophy to make sure that Professor Kåre Øy was there. It was a quarter past four. The departmental secretary had told me that he generally drove home around five.

During the preceding few months I'd begun studying philosophy on my own and reading textbooks written for doctors specializing in psychiatry. I wanted to try to understand why human beings, regardless of background, indulge in violation. Øy had been interviewed on the subject some weeks earlier in the *Aftenposten*. I didn't know anyone else I could talk to. I suppressed the nagging feeling that the professor might have better things to do than talk to me.

I was an ardent proponent of Marxism and historical materialism. They helped me make sense of events in my own chaotic era. I wanted to change the world and fight against the repression of the majority of the world's population.

My problem was that Marxist classics never discussed the possibility that injustice might be used in the very name of Marxism. They even shied away from discussing the term 'ethics'. A constant stream of gruesome revelations from Cuba and China troubled me. The aggressors were convinced that they represented progress and the interests of humanity, just as many of the psychiatrists, nurses and psychologists at my own workplace did. They also believed they could pigeonhole the individual and describe how everybody thought. Each person, each patient, received a diagnosis and that determined the drugs' regime, the surgical operations, the interventions. I was twenty-three and wondered if these people, who seemed so sure and thought they understood the whole human being, found it easier to violate than those who had doubts.

And what about me? For several years I'd despised myself because of a faulty chromosome. Wasn't that a kind of violation, too? I needed help. Outside Gaustad. Kåre Øy was the man I needed to speak to. He was a philosopher and from what I understood, he was best fitted to explain what constituted transgression against another individual.

I locked up my bike outside the Department of History and took the lift to the sixth floor.

In the lift I stared into a large mirror. I was red in the face and sweaty. What on earth was I doing? I hadn't even been told that he'd see me. I brushed a hand across my nylon trousers to make sure the paint was dry. The lift stopped, I took one last glance at the mirror, before stepping hesitantly into a long, poorly lit corridor. The walls were red brick, the ceiling black with oblong light fittings that exuded a dim light. At the end of the passage was a large window with a view of Tryvann telecommunications tower and the forests of Nordmarka.

The door nearest the window had his name on it. There was no one about. I bent my head and put my ear to the door. Had he left already? I noticed that the round clock near the lift stood at twenty to five. I knocked. I heard a 'yes'. The voice sounded irritated. For an instant it stuck me that Øy might have been hoping to work in peace for a couple of hours. In order to dissipate the thought I knocked again. This time a little more cautiously. When there was no answer, I opened the door a fraction.

Kåre Øy was standing with his back to me staring out of the window. His left hand grasped the edge of a large, untidy desk. In the middle of the desk, before the empty chair, lay a pile of typewritten sheets.

'I can come another time,' I said turning in the doorway.

'It's too late.'

'I didn't mean to disturb you,' I said.

'*I didn't mean to disturb you*,' he repeated.

He wore brown shoes and a white shirt. His trousers were held up with black braces. His jacket hung over the back of a chair by a small table to the left of the door. He was short and very slight. His hair was grey and wavy. Øy turned slowly in the big office and looked at me. He put on a pair of black horn-rimmed glasses which lay on the desk.

'You're a student here?'

I shook my head and gave my name, told him where I worked, and that I was grateful he'd let me see him, that I was studying philosophy on my own account because I wanted to understand the causes of injustice.

I realized I was going into rather too much detail.

Øy sighed. Or did I simply imagine it?

'I've read some of the works of people such as Immanuel Kant and Søren Kierkegaard,' I said.

There was almost fifteen metres between us. He remained standing. So did I.

'Sit down there. You said you're working?'

He pointed to the table by the door.

'Write four sides on what you've understood of Immanuel Kant's concept *das Ding an sich*. There a biro and paper there. You've got sixty minutes.'

We sat each at our own desk. Occasionally he got up, glanced at me, wrote a few words, crossed out, wrote, shook his head, sighed, stretched his arms above his head. I took my time; he appeared to have forgotten both it and me.

When I'd finished, he took the sheets.

'You haven't grasped very much of this. You must study general works before starting on the originals.'

He recommended a few titles.

'Thank you,' I said. 'Can you help me understand what causes us to be unjust? Could you be my instructor?'

'I can't give an opinion on that just now. You must enrol in the university, then we'll see.'

'I need to get going, I must have help.'

I thought I could discern a kind of disquiet in the small face with its green eyes.

'Remember that we are all predisposed to commit the grosser violations. What people often forget is that the vast majority of us are guilty of injustice on a daily basis. We don't acknowledge that we're different from the people around us. We scorn the idea that we're not normal, without having the faintest idea of what normality is. As human beings we are self-destructive.'

Going down in the lift, I looked into the mirror and wondered if he could read my thoughts, or if there was something in my appearance which proclaimed my past.

I carried the picnic hamper. Sunniva had a couple of rolled-up rugs over her shoulder. She was wearing a big straw hat with a red ribbon. We were among the first to stake our place on the green grass of Sofienberg Park that Saturday. It was the summer holidays and more than six years since we'd met at Gaustad. We 'd written to each other during the years she studied geology at Tromsø. Now we'd become lovers.

The weather forecast the previous evening had promised temperatures approaching 30°C. The park would get crowded. It was already so warm that I asked whether we oughtn't to get closer to Sofienberg Church where there was more shade. Sunniva shook her head. Surely I could tolerate that, how many sunny days were there in the course of a Norwegian summer? I looked at her. She smiled.

'One,' I said.

Sunniva kissed me. Sunbathing had been her idea. I'd have been happy with a walk in the forest. I'd given in when she volunteered to make the food and fill a thermos.

After a coffee and two sandwiches I had to admit that a lazy day on the grass was both peaceful and pleasing. Perhaps there was something in what Sunniva and others had pointed out, that occasionally it might be good for me to relax completely. I lay on my back wearing black bathing shorts that accentuated my paleness. Sunniva had covered me with sun cream, and now she asked me to rub hers in. She lay on her stomach in a yellow bikini, brown and beautiful. I knelt and massaged her neck, shoulders, her strong spine, the small, downy fair hairs in the small of her back, her thighs and calves.

Sunniva laid aside the article she was reading about new finds and the origin of rock formations in Scandinavia, closed her eyes and sighed a couple of times before turning her face towards me and pouting. Afterwards I lay down on my back again. She sat up and edged up close to me, blotting out the sun so that I could see her face. She stroked my chest and said that she'd noticed I didn't want to turn on my front.

'Your shoulder blades aren't so weird that you can't lie on your stomach for half an hour.'

'OK,' I said and rolled over.

She stroked my hair and shifted so that the sun fell on me.

'Hey.'

'Um?' I said turning my face towards her.

'I think I'm pregnant.'

I sat up quickly and stared across at the tallest tree in the park. I tried to say something, but I couldn't get anything out.

She kissed me on the forehead and took both my hands.

Seconds passed.

'I told you that my illness is hereditary,' I said.

I heard how disjointed and odd my words sounded.

'You've got other characteristics too,' she said.

She smiled.

I let go of her hands.

'D'you want this child?'

My voice was frantic.

'I wanted a termination at first. But not now.'

I shook my head.

'I'm scared of letting you down,' I said.

'You've got responsibilities, too,' Sunniva said. 'It's your child I want to have, not someone else's.'

'When must you decide? About an abortion, I mean.'

'The cut-off point's later if one of the parents has a hereditary disease.'

She brushed her hand across her face and regarded me.

'Look at me,' she said.

I lifted my gaze.

'I don't know if I want you to have it,' I said.

'Pull yourself together,' she replied.

She enfolded me in her arms.

We kissed, smiled, kissed again, looked around, spread her rug over us and stopped talking.

The fly, roused from its hibernation, lands on the black-currant-syrup stain on the floor next to me.

Its wings are ragged. Its body sags slightly at the back, the wings pointing out into the room.

The fly's got that shiny-worn, greenish gleam of elderly house flies.

Its legs have so little spring in them that the last joint is invisible.

The fly gathers its strength, soon its wings begin to beat, slowly at first, then faster.

It tries to take off.

The fly gives up and sits motionless.

It takes longer and longer rests between each new attempt.

Its head is brown and hairy, like a coconut.

It stretches backwards and forwards and flexes its legs as if to launch itself just as its wings vibrate vigorously.

When a wing or a leg has managed to liberate itself, the other wing and leg sink deeper into the syrup.

At another attempt it crashes during a feeble forward leap.

It lands on its belly, head first, with its front legs stretched out.

Its eyes are barely visible, do they open and close?

Is it something I'm imagining?

My phone lights up and vibrates on the shelf.

It could be *Dagsavisen* wondering what's become of the article I was going to write.

Imagine if the vibration caused it to fall off the edge?

My personal alarm lies next to it, barely visible.

I stare at the ceiling and at my phone by turns.

It rings again.

It lights up.

Numbers I cannot clearly see, flash up and vanish.

When you lose something you love, you can die of sorrow.

A person, a dog, a body.

It happens because the left ventricle swells up.

It takes on an entirely new shape, not unlike that of a pitcher.

The Japanese call the condition *takotsubo*, the name of a very special pitcher with a large body and a narrow neck.

Japanese seamen use it to catch squid.

The squid squeezes inside but can't work out how to escape.

I had invited Karoline to the Symra Cinema to see the premiere of *Alice in Wonderland*. She asked if Sunniva was coming too. I said she had to go to a meeting, and that it would be nice if we could do something together. As the cinema was close by, it wouldn't take long to drive there. Furthermore, there was a disabled parking space right by the entrance.

The cinema had been renovated and enlarged, as had the rest of the Lambertseter Centre. The show could be viewed using 3D glasses. We bought them at the entrance. Neither of us had tried this before.

Karoline had just started sixth-form college, and I wasn't using a wheelchair at the time, even though my occupational therapist had recommended one.

I noticed that my legs felt numb and that the distance between the comfortable car seat and the auditorium was further than I'd been expecting. Karoline, who'd been steering and supporting me for those fifty metres, probably found the deterioration in my condition just as much of a surprise as it was to me.

We had to get to row 14, seats 23 and 24. She went first.

I looked over and spotted the two vacant seats, some distance away. To get to them, I had to turn towards the people who were already seated in the row.

I moved sideways by pushing my right foot to the right and then dragging my left foot after it. It worked well the first time. I forced my right foot to the right using my thigh and calf. Once shoe and foot were in the right position, I transferred my weight on to the heel and sole. I raised my left foot slightly so that the shoe would slide more easily.

It was important that it didn't get caught up in the shoes of those who were already seated. The fourth time I drew my left leg in, pain shot through my hip, just where the neck of the femur joins the pelvis.

To keep my balance, I had to steady myself on those sitting in front of me. As I passed the first four people, I placed my right hand on their left shoulders. By the time I got to seat number 13, I'd lost all control of what my right hand was grasping. By the end, I had no sensation in my legs at all. They could have given way at any moment.

Karoline had already sat down and was looking straight ahead—at the advertisement.

As I slumped into my seat, the man sitting next to me enquired:

'Do you come here often?'

'Three times a week,' I replied. 'There's no cinema in town like it for acoustics.'

Only then did it strike me that he might have asked the question in order to deflect attention from my rather awkward entrance, and that the words were kindly meant. I didn't know how to develop the subject, so I sat there staring ahead of me.

As the auditorium went dark, just before the film began, Karoline leant towards me and whispered that I'd been in a clinch with an elderly man who was her maths teacher, a girl in her class and the woman who worked on the till in the corner store.

'Perhaps we could go to a cinema a bit further from home next time?' she said as the film corporation's fanfare blared out.

Karoline threw her arms around my neck and stroked my crew cut.

'Lovely to see you, Dad!'

I hadn't set eyes on her for five months. Her degree in history at Uppsala was finished. Now she was going to a bedsit in the University of Oslo's hall of residence while studying for her masters in Oslo.

Karoline seated herself at the dining table. She'd never seen me in a wheelchair before. She looked as if she might be about to say something but decided against it, so she reached for the bread basket and appraised the spreads I'd put out. Her eyes quickly registered her favourites, the same ones she'd liked since play school. She spoke eagerly about the USA's foreign policy since the war.

I examined her face as she talked. The minute muscles on the right side of her mouth had deteriorated since I'd seen her last. I recognized the signs. The same thing had happened to me when I was twenty-two. When she wanted to take a slice of cheese, she used the slicer at an angle. I do it myself. When I last saw her she'd used the slicer straight, in the normal way.

I cut at an angle because the muscles in my right shoulder don't work like they used to. Consciously or unconsciously you search for new movements to compensate for the original ones. She seemed unfazed, she was on automatic pilot. I began to wonder how many movements I and my body have adapted during the course of my life to replace the first learnt movements. I wondered if it would be appropriate to mention how marvellously the body adjusts to the new reality when it loses some of its original functions. The theme would have been a relevant one. It made me think about her future, once Sunniva and I are gone. Even though we know more about the disease now than when I was a boy, and stem cell research is making great strides, I feared future attitudes to what was normal and what wasn't.

'How did it go at Grandma's?' Karoline enquired. 'Would she say anything about her father and the family?'

'Nothing much. What I need is more material about my grandfather to get her to open up. I'm finding it hard going.'

Karoline stroked my arm. She mentioned that Christine Wood, the mother of a student friend of hers, who worked as a search room assistant at the Oslo City Archives, might possibly be able to help.

I thanked her for the tip and passed her the orange juice.

'Karoline, I've got some other rather bad news. Grandma's got cancer but she won't talk about it.'

'How awful, Dad.'

She leant forward, covered her face with her hand and let out a deep sigh.

'It's sad, even though she's old,' I said.

She gave me a worried look. 'I'll visit her. She needs comforting.'

'Try by all means.'

Karoline raised her head. Her eyes were moist.

'When I came I was looking forward to telling you a rather sweet story. Perhaps now's not the time . . . ?'

'You just tell me anyway,' I said.

One of her fellow Norwegian students, who'd smuggled a hip flask into the vice chancellor's reception for successful undergraduates, had got drunk. When his hip flask was empty, the student went over to the table where the white wine bottles stood in their coolers. He was refused a drink. The student grabbed a wine cooler, which was light enough for him to lift, and drank the cold water. Several ice cubes fell on the floor. The water poured over him before he placed it back on the table.

It was marvellous to have a laugh together.

'I knew you'd like it,' she said.

When Karoline was ten, I'd asked her what I should do if I could have an injection to make me completely well again. 'But then you wouldn't be my daddy any more,' she replied, 'you'd be someone else.'

When we'd finished eating, she poured tea for us both using her new shoulder movement.

Did I feel a kind of sorrow?

Karoline leant forward, looked into my eyes and said that in a bygone age, quite a few children would almost certainly have been killed because their parents wouldn't have known how to deal with a disability.

'At least that doesn't happen now,' she said.

'Now it's dealt with in a different way,' I said. 'Once a disability is discovered, it's frequently weeded out. Many people see that as progress.'

Karoline squeezed my hand: 'I'm alive right here and now. You are too,' she said. 'Don't be so pessimistic.'

I would have liked so much to take her in my arms and say: *You're so right*, and hug her again. But I didn't.

I'm thirsty.

I shove my right elbow under my torso.

I manage that, but I can't raise my hip and pull my right leg towards me so that I can get up on all fours.

The leg barely moves.

I try with my left.

During the attempt I feel the pain in what's left of my long thigh muscle.

If it's stressed too much, it'll tear.

I move my left leg slowly.

I shift my foot a few inches and push my hip up as hard as I can.

There's a pressure at my temples and over my eyes.

Why aren't I feeling more hungry? Is it fear that's suppressing my appetite?

I am meat in the darkness.

At last I succeed in raising my hip off the floor a little.

Numbly, my left arm tries to prop up my trunk.

My stomach muscles can't help me, they disappeared years ago.

Even so, I try again.

And again.

What is it that's driving me on?

Despite all the defeats, despite its six hundred and fifty muscles ceasing to work one after another, my body won't give in to the force that inexorably drives it towards the earth's innermost core.

I don't know what made me walk for the first time.

I was, allegedly, ten months old and standing next to the rickety green stool in my grandmother's kitchen.

I gazed around, altered my grip and turned my head towards the utility sink.

I released my hold and took my first steps, and then fell and began to cry.

I try to lift my hip and pull my left leg under me once again, I raise my upper body, I push my palms against the floor and straighten my arms.

They shake with the effort.

My heart is pumping as fast as it can, in and out of the right and left ventricles.

Up, up.

Up and stand.

Walk, walk.

THIRD SUNDAY IN ADVENT

The taxi driver wheels me in and positions me beside my mother's kitchen table, like last time.

Is it my imagination, or is she looking more tired than she was a fortnight ago?

Yes, she's even more drawn and pale.

Although I want to try to tease out more information, I realize that knowing she's terminally ill has blunted some of the determination I'd felt the last time I was here.

'So you've come back?' she says nodding.

I hold out my hand to her. She takes it briefly.

'We agreed,' I reply.

The table is laid as usual, with brie, biscuits in a basket, cups, small plates, thermos, knives. Even the spreads are the same as a fortnight ago. The only difference is a few paper napkins with a puppy motif on them. Mother says that she's bought the napkins to support the Norwegian Association for the Blind. I nod when she asks if I want coffee. She pours for both of us. We sip and swallow.

My gaze wanders between my mother's face and the tree outside. We eat biscuits and cheese in silence. I imagine us as characters in a film set in the American south, where the heat outside is unbearable, and the fan on the ceiling chops at the heavy air without making it any fresher, just sends it back to us, leaving us feeling as listless as before.

'Didn't you want Sunniva and me to have children, Mother?'

'That was up to you.'

'That's true.'

'Of course I wanted grandchildren.'

'Even though?'

My mother looks at me, before lowering her head. Her veiled eyelids indicate that her focus is on a spot close to her hands. She holds them between her stomach and her breasts, twining and twisting the fingers like a living knot. I imagine her sitting here like this even after I've gone. Perhaps she's brooding about death or transience? Perhaps she's thinking about what she'll do with the letters and photographs in front of her? Mother was always working on something. Could a kind of melancholy have possessed her? It's possible that the sight of the piles in front of her make her think that these last crumbs of her time on earth are just enough to keep alive the sense of loss for what had once been.

'D'you think we should have followed your example and not talked to Karoline once it became apparent that she'd got the illness?'

'If I'd started talking, it . . . '

My mother looks out, blankly, as if she hasn't said any-thing at all.

'Then add something, Mother, something that can be understood, give the words some meaning.'

She's breathing heavily.

'Should I have remained silent when Karoline looked in the mirror and saw that something was wrong?'

She clears her throat.

'Silence can be as painful as blows or kicks, Mother. It can do a lot of damage.'

She fixes her gaze on something behind me.

'That's why I chose to talk to Karoline,' I persist.

'How clever you are,' she says without looking at me.

'Maybe I put it a bit clumsily, but now Karoline knows that she's got someone to talk to when things become painful or difficult. Isn't that nice to know as a grandmother?'

I sit there hoping that my mother will find it easier to talk about her grandchild than about our relationship. At the very least it may provide the opportunity to say something more general.

'Mother, when I had my diagnosis, it was a shock, but there's one thing I've always been grateful for.'

Her eyes seek out mine.

'It's that the doctor told it as it was, even though I was only fifteen and the subject was a bleak one. The fact that he trusted me and treated me as the "grown-up" person I then imagined I was, led to his continuing as my doctor for the rest of his life.'

'I didn't know he was dead.'

'That's strange, you read the obituaries.'

'I must have missed it,' she says smoothing the tablecloth.

I can't think tactically or hold myself back any longer.

'Was it that Grandma persuaded your father to take care of himself when he got worse? Did Grandma say anything to you about it? Surely you and your brother talked it over? It's one thing for Grandma to take you and leave Tor, but there's something I don't understand—I can't find your brother on the national register after you and Grandma left Grandfather in Elvegata. What happened?'

I can hear that I'm breathing hard.

'No one ever spared me,' she puts in.

'In what way?'

'I've said enough.'

'You haven't said anything at all.'

'As you like.'

'What became of Uncle Frode from the age of fourteen? What did you and Grandma keep silent about?'

'You're indulging in wild speculation,' she says, her voice rising.

'Yes, that's exactly what it is. Then say something, tell me something different, so I don't have to speculate. While you don't talk I'll keep on finding new questions.'

'Don't dig around in all this before I'm gone.'

'Mother, there's more chance of surviving cancer treatment now than in the old days. I've told Karoline that you're ill. She's terribly upset.'

'It's over now.'

'You're not going to try?'

'That,' she says, 'is something for me to decide.'

Several seconds go by.

'I was engaged before I met your father,' she says at last.

I'd never heard this before, not from her or anyone else. I assume she can read in my face just how flabbergasted I am. I had no idea she'd had a love life before she met my father. How naive of me.

'Did you love him?' I ask.

She mumbles something I can't decipher. I find I'm not able to ask the man's name, much less if she loved Father when they got engaged two years later.

'My fiancé met Frode by chance and noticed that he was . . . different.'

'You mean he was walking rather like I did before I used a wheelchair?'

Mother nods.

'After that I saw Frode as little as possible.'

'How often?'

'Three times, in connection with Grandma's will.'

'Because you were angry with him?'

'I didn't want to see him again.'

'D'you think your fiancé broke off the engagement because he realized that you could pass on a hereditary disease?'

She bangs the table so hard that the cups rattle.

'I've said too much already. I shouldn't have said anything at all.'

I straighten first her cup and then my own, so that they stand centred in their saucers once more.

When Frode was fifteen years younger than I am now, he was helped about by Eline and others, not only in Bogstad-veien but also to the insurance company office in Grensen where he'd got a job as it was impossible for him to work as a painter.

I'm on the point of asking my mother what she did if they met by chance in the street or elsewhere. The face in front of me looks so weary that I desist. Eline and Frode may have felt betrayed when they passed, and Mother may have felt contempt. I don't enquire about this, either.

'Did you go to Frode's funeral?'

'No,' my mother replies, twisting her wedding ring.

I've always been fascinated by things in the air: ski jumpers, divers, birds, planes, airships, rockets, stars and planets, and the Northern Lights.

I've seen bits of meteorites the size of a stone that you could hold in one hand.

They were formed four and a half billion years ago.

They usually land in the wilds or in the sea.

Last August I saw a meteorite crater on Ekeberg plain.

The meteorite's journey began in the asteroid belt between Mars and Jupiter, and ended in a hollow twenty-two centimetres square on the plain.

The hole was two hundred and fourteen metres from the concrete foundations of the mast where the airship *Norge* was moored on the 14th of April 1926, ready for its voyage across the North Pole.

I sat in my wheelchair outside the Oslo City Archives waiting for Christine Wood, the mother of Karoline's student friend. The occasional snowflake landed on my oilskin jacket and black Levi's trousers. Where on earth was she? I tried to think about something else.

The interval between the time Karoline was fourteen, when we'd looked at one another in the mirror—and now, is history. The interval between the moment Dr Lachmann gave me my diagnosis—and now, is also history.

The snow continued to sift down.

It was fifteen minutes since the taxi driver had dropped me off. Could I have misunderstood? Was it twelve thirty and not midday that Christine had said? Wet snow blew on to my face and at the red-brick building behind me. The pavement had got a covering of snow while I'd been waiting.

I took off a glove and squeezed my jacket to check that my mobile was there in my inside pocket.

Perhaps half past twelve *was* what we'd agreed? My watch said it was 12.21. A black-and-white pointer came running up and began sniffing. It shook off the snowflakes. I patted it. It lifted its back leg. I yelled. The stream missed my boots by an inch. The dog ran off in the direction of Uelandsgate.

I had information about my grandfather, Tor, but getting the data to make sense required words and sentences.

We—Grandma, Mother and I—had crawled sideways through time like crabs, contemplating the details we'd added to our narrative about Tor.

Melting snow was on the point of seeping into my trousers.

My mobile rang. It was after half past twelve. I assumed it was Karoline, she was probably wondering if Christine and I had found anything out. I undid the zip of my jacket and tugged at my scarf to reach the phone. It stopped ringing before I could get hold of it.

Could Christine Wood have forgotten our appointment?

When Sunniva and I decided to have the baby, we couldn't be certain just how the disease would develop. No two case histories are alike. In this knowledge lay a kernel of hope, stemming the notion that problems would almost certainly arise sooner or later. Or was the truth even more banal? Did I believe my will was stronger than the disease? Deep within me lay the hope that the destruction of cells within my body would cease. After finding love, I was suffused with an optimism about the future for which I really had no foundation.

It's possible that Karoline will reproach me one day for what I said that time we stood in front of the mirror after she'd discovered what was happening to her: *Things will work out*, I'd said, as if I'd had some sort of guarantee.

'There you are!'

I turned. A tall woman in a white shirt and round, red glasses, was proffering a hand and smiling.

'I'm Christine, sorry, I tried to ring you, I thought you weren't coming, this isn't the best entrance for a wheelchair, you see. But there's warmth and coffee inside,' she said as large snowflakes fell wetly on her black curls.

Lithe and elegant, even in her slippery black shoes, she manoeuvred me inside and then on to an office where she helped me off with my jacket and hung it up to dry. My scarf and cap were placed on bench in front of the heater. The time was ten to one. She said she had plenty of time.

'Good,' I mumbled as she wheeled me into a larger room, with computer terminals and several rows of tables where one could sit and pour over the archives. I told her about the conversation I'd had with my mother ten days before.

Christine promised to help me find the sources I needed.

She gave me a tour of the Archive Department's digital services, including scanned church registers, directories and probate documents—and the City Archives' own library: twenty thousand metres of shelves containing historical material, like records of births and deaths and various Oslo city censuses in which one could 'follow the citizens' movements throughout their lives, to use Christine's own words. In addition, she thought that as *Aftenposten* had digitalized its editions right back to 1860, there'd be plenty for us to search for. It was Wednesday. She'd be able to assist me all the rest of today, Thursday and half of Friday. I thanked her.

The first thing Christine taught me was how to search *Aftenposten* digitally using my grandfather's name. After a few minutes it brought up an advertisement he'd placed. It was headed: *Has anybody lost a gold pocket watch?* Grandfather had found it and wanted the rightful owner to have it back. I felt ashamed of myself for thinking that maybe he hadn't found the watch at all but had taken it, and then had a guilty conscience.

After two days in the City Archives I was beginning to get some idea of who my grandfather was.

The year is 1926. The city census shows that Tor, Grandma and the children are living in a house in Nesoddtangen. The house still stands. The centre of Oslo was forty minutes away by boat. Christine discovered that Tor was a member of the local yacht club, and that he had various business interests. Among other things, he was an agent for steel brushes. When my mother was four, they moved. Tor's financial circumstances had worsened considerably. The family were now living in rundown accommodation in Elvegata. The newspapers of the day described the area as a slum. The timber building stood on Akerselva's lower reaches, just before the river spills out into Oslofjord. Small cargo boats carried coal, building materials and a variety of small goods up and down the brown river. Christine showed me several old pictures of the area. Rats, open sewers, bad water and disease were rife. The area has now been completely cleared. Their social descent must have been a long one. The children went to Vaterland School, which no longer exists either. Three years later Tor was living alone in the flat in Elvegata. After another couple of years he no longer appeared under any address.

The National Archives' Probate register provides the explanation.

Grandfather died alone, aged forty-eight, on 13th of December 1939. The police found him on the floor in a room near Stortorget. The Register of Deaths gives the cause as cerebral haemorrhage after a fall. According to the Register he possessed *no worldly goods*.

Christine gave me a map from the Interment Department. The map shows the entire cemetery, with an arrow showing where Tor's grave had been. According to the Department the grave site was 'erased', as no one had paid the ground rent since the turn of the millennium.

Next day Sunniva suggested a visit to the cemetery. We took the map that Christine had copied. The site of Grandfather's grave was only a stone's throw from Grandma's. A large rhododendron now grew where the stone had once stood. Three tall spruce trees swayed above the rhododendron.

I reversed a little so that I could see the tops of the spruce trees. The tallest of them might be twenty metres high. The lower branches were so dense that the snow hadn't fallen on the ground but blown in under them, covering the frosty green and brown grass.

Who was Grandma? She dressed well, always wore a skirt, usually plain blouses or tops, and wore a hat when she went out. Her eyes were green, her hair had once been brown, she was slim and she suffered from rheumatism in later life, something that could be discerned from her increasingly crooked fingers. The general opinion was that Grandma hadn't the striking good looks of her daughter, but she was more serene. I'd often been in the back seat of the car when my father drove Grandma home after Sunday lunch. On one occasion we were involved in a collision on a slippery winter road; on another we found ourselves at a police check only to discover that my father had forgotten his driving licence. Both times Father banged the steering wheel and I covered my face with my hands. But Grandma lit a cigarette, gazed out of the window and remarked that things could have been worse.

After the meeting with Christine Wood, I spent the whole weekend trying to write down everything I'd learnt. On Monday morning I phoned her with a question. When Grandma and Mother left Tor, did Grandma take Frode with her or did he remain in Elvegata—or was there some other explanation?

A couple of hours later Christine had the answer. According to the census, Uncle Frode had lived in north Oslo. She paused before giving me the address. It was a home for boys, particularly orphans. Its regulations, as I read on Google afterwards, stated that 'spastics' and 'the insane' were not welcome. The institution was run on pietistic and Lutheran principles. Its rules sanctioned the use of corporal punishment. Discipline, schoolwork and Bible studies were considered the foundation of the boys' education. The best behaved could sing at funerals or work in the home's own printing press. It was only after Frode's death that various forms of abuse been uncovered at the home, from what I could glean on the internet.

After spending eighteen months at the home, Frode was taken on by a Fred Olsen ship plying to Newcastle. He was fifteen.

I phoned Eline and told her what I'd found out. What had her father said about the boys' home and about life at sea? Was it his decision to become a seaman?

I was so eager that my cousin could hardly get a word in for the first few minutes. I had to apologize.

Her father had mentioned the boys' home to Eline, but he'd never spoken about the time he'd spent there. He was away at sea for three years, and when he came home for good, his mother had married again, to a man who, like Tor, had built up his own business. Her husband had begun as a waiter, then rose in the trade until he finally became the joint owner of a medium-sized restaurant.

Eline said she'd got a number of letters and photos left by her father, Frode. They were in their storage locker in the cellar. She told me that 'perhaps one day' she'd look at them.

I asked if she'd like to visit me. There was silence at the other end of the phone.

'It would be lovely to meet after all this time,' I said.

'Yes,' she said at last.

Eline arrived the next day at one o'clock. She had an evening shift at the National Hospital where she worked as a biotechnician.

The front door had hardly shut behind her before she was staring at me transfixed. 'It's just like looking at Dad.'

I sat in my wheelchair and examined her figure and face. She was tall, she must have been five foot ten, and dark. There was little similarity between us apart from our noses and a quiff of hair on the right side of our heads. Her eyes were brown. Eline smiled warmly. She asked if there was somewhere she could hang her coat. I chattered on about the weather and said I'd heard it was slippery outside. She made no comment. Eline had brought a plastic bag with her. I showed her into the living room.

On the table stood a jug of apple juice and two glasses, and a box of Anton Berg chocolates. I waved in their direction and said that there was a jug of apple juice with two glasses, and a box of chocolates there, as if she were blind.

Eline followed me to the table. I indicated where I wanted her to sit. She seated herself as we took one another in.

She held out her hand.

I held out my hand.

'Perhaps we should say hello,' Eline said.

'Yes, perhaps we should.'

She got up and came round the table.

We embraced.

'It's high time,' she said.

'It is high time,' I said.

The bag she'd brought along contained a number of photographs of her parents, mainly of her father, she told me. Grandma was in one, taken at Eline's confirmation. I asked if she had more pictures of her. She shook her head and took out some letters that I could borrow.

'Have you read them?' I asked.

'Yes, at long last. I'm not sure but I think that it was all to do with shame as far as Grandma and your mum were concerned.'

She placed the bag on my lap and took out the black-and-white photos that lay on top.

'Can you see the likeness between my father and yourself?' she asked.

'Oh yes, the large head, the forehead, the cheekbones, the hairline—even the chin is similar.'

Eline nodded.

'I feel a great loss,' I went on, 'at never having known about the man who was such an important part of our history. We've both lived in the same city and must have passed each other on various occasions without my being acquainted with you and your parents.'

After Eline had gone, I began to read Frode's letters. Most of them were about his time at sea and the years immediately after. Eline had found the letters when she was sorting through her father's things after his death. Visits to cities like New York, Los Angeles and Buenos Aires recur, but there's also frequent descriptions of certain members of the crew. Especially Sixten Ohlson, a Swedish ship's engineer who'd married a Norwegian woman and lived in Marselisgate in Oslo's Grünerløkka. He was the one who'd taught Frode to play chess. When Ohlson shipped on another vessel, they began to correspond, Eline had informed me. Ohlson's widow returned the letters to Frode after Sixten passed away.

While at sea, Frode decided that he wanted to enrol at the Oslo College of Maritime Studies. *The college is like a palace dominating the capital and the fjord from its hillside at Ekeberg,* he says in one letter.

I think that, by and large, Frode's life at sea was a happy time. The change came when he decided to go ashore.

He wrote to Ohlson that the possibility of training as a telegraph operator 'would have to wait'.

Frode had visited his mother and stepfather and told them of his dream of becoming a telegraphist. He asked them for a loan to pay for his training. It wasn't forthcoming. His mother thought that working as a seaman wasn't a suitable job for Frode. His stepfather offered him a job washing dishes in the restaurant he partly owned. If Frode did well, he could progress to a job as a waiter.

In the same letter, Frode went on to say that he was worried he'd contracted the same disease as his father: *There's something worrying me, Sixten. I've started dragging my right foot just very slightly, the way I remember my father doing.*

I ran my index finger under the words again and read them aloud. A thought insinuated itself and displaced all the others that clamoured for attention. I hesitated a few moments before picking up my mobile and dialling Eline.

I thanked her for visiting me and asked if her father had ever told her where he was when Grandfather Tor died.

'I don't like talking about it,' Eline said.

'I'd be very grateful if you could all the same,' I replied.

A few months before his father died, Frode wrote to him. There was no answer. Frode became worried. The last time he had shore leave in the capital, his father was having difficulty walking, and also Frode couldn't see how his father got money for basic necessities, according to Eline.

'I assume that was what Dad had in the back of his mind when, as a nineteen-year-old, he went to visit our granddad,' she said.

Frode went up the back stairs to the door on the second floor of the house in Elvegata and knocked. He got no answer. After a while a neighbour, a woman, opened her door and told him that Tor had been dead for several months.

It went quiet at the other end of the line.

'What did your father do then?' I asked.

'I think he always blamed himself for not keeping in closer contact with his dad.'

'Did he say anything about that?'

'Very little. Odd remarks. *Terrible. Awful.* No more than that.'

'Do you know where he went after receiving that message from the neighbour?'

'He went back to the married couple in Marselisgate and stayed there for several weeks. Sixten got him a job as a painter. Dad always spoke well of Sixten and Turid,' Eline said.

I'm in a dream. It's a good place to be. It's midsummer and hot. I can see a hedge nearby, grass, scattered flowers coloured red, orange, violet, pink, brown, white, blue, mauve, turquoise, indigo, and a large maple with ashen-brown boughs and green leaves. I walk barefoot over to the wicker chair beneath the shade of the branches, and sit down.

I cross my legs, stretch my arms in the air before settling them on the armrests.

There's no one in sight. I grasp my lips and try to purse them, like a whistler would. I look around again to make sure I'm alone. Almost imperceptibly at first, and then with greater effort, I attempt to force a sound from between my flaccid lips. I try four times.

From the hedge emerge five hedgehogs, two sparrows, seven snails, one white cat and a couple of small grey mice. They settle down beneath my chair. My legs are still crossed.

I stretch my left arm.

My fingers reach down to my knee.

It's still tender.

It's a good thing I didn't fall outside.

Out there I might have frozen to death.

Let's hope the electricity doesn't fail.

If it does, the generator will take over.

Actually, I've never asked the caretaker if we have one.

The power once went during a heart operation at a hospital in western Norway.

When they eventually found the generator, it didn't work.

I flex my left leg, reach down with both my arms and clasp my hands behind the knee.

The fingers knit together.

It hurts, but I manage to stretch my back.

I raise my head, stretch my neck muscles and turn my face from left to right, and then the other way.

There's a pain in my shoulders, my hands release their grip and my calf, the back of my knee and my thigh slap to the floor.

I try to raise my right knee.

The leg has gone to sleep.

I try to wake it up, tugging at my trousers to bring life to my thigh bone, kneecap and shin.

I manage to get the knee a couple of inches from the floor before it thumps down again.

Beneath my clothes there is 1.8 square metres of skin stretched over five litres of blood, thirteen billion nerve cells and twenty-five billion red blood corpuscles.

I've got twenty-three pairs of chromosomes in each cell.

The chromosomes in each pair are the same length, apart from the fourth. There, one of the chromosomes is fractionally shorter than the other.

That's why I can't get up and walk out of this text.

THIRD SUNDAY IN ADVENT

A tiny dust mote in front of me eddies around a solitary sunbeam. While I struggle to find words for the new discoveries in the archives, it strikes me that there is something lofty and unapproachable about my mother. It makes her similar in some way to the angel in the lead-glass picture that hangs in front of the living-room window. I mention the association, but it makes no impression.

Suddenly she leans forward and reaches under the table. She brings out a plastic bottle of brass polish which she'll use on the three-branched candelabra. She reads the instructions on the back out loud.

Father was the one who taught me that you should never be frightened to ask questions about things you didn't understand. Apart from the thing we never talked about. My father may have hoped, or been advised, that the illness might not manifest itself. Perhaps he didn't want to cause me needless anxiety? When it became clear that I'd inherited the disease, it must have been hard for him, to say the very least, to admit that he'd known about the possibility but had hoped for the best. What would Sunniva and Karoline say about my persistent questioning when it was obvious my mother had got worse? There were several times during the past fortnight when I'd realized I needed more answers, and that maybe for her, telling it as it was at last might feel like some sort of resolution. But I also realized that others might disagree.

'Did you and Father agree not to talk to me about my illness and your secret family?'

'Yes.'

I'm about to say that she's lied to me before, but I manage to hold my tongue.

Whatever the truth, it was my father's responsibility to talk to me, when we were alone on our skiing trips, for example. He could have helped me to accept the body I was born with. It might have forged a bond between us and helped me deal with the increasing pain and the difficult thoughts of puberty. The fact that he said nothing, reinforced the destructive impulses within me.

'Don't drag you father into this,' my mother adds raising her plate and bringing it down again, hard. 'It's bad enough that you harbour those notions about me, but you can at least spare *him*.'

'You were both in it together,' I reply.

She shrugs her shoulders.

'You think that honesty always pays?' she says.

'After I was diagnosed, I imagined how my arms, legs, hips and the rest of my body would deteriorate bit by bit. When there isn't anyone willing to talk about it at home, you can imagine how hard it is to turn to others. I couldn't talk to either of you,' I persist, 'not to you or Father. Shame and self-contempt were my only reference points in those first years after my diagnosis.'

Her eyes stare straight ahead. The pale fingers enclose the warm cup.

Just then I notice a smell I wasn't aware of before.

'What's that burnt smell, Mother?'

'I burnt some food yesterday evening. I expect the smell will go soon. There won't be any Christmas party this year,' she adds evenly.

'Is this something you've just decided, or had you made up your mind a long time ago?'

'I think it's best this way.'

'But Karoline will be . . . '

What can I say?

' . . . disappointed.'

'That's enough now.'

I can make do without the party, but Karoline, even though she's grown up, will be upset. Tradition is important to her, and she knows how much the gathering has meant to her grandmother.

'Have you thought about telling her?' I enquire.

'I thought you could do that,' says my mother. 'You'll find an excuse, if I know you. Well, do you feel like a Pils? I'm tired of tea and coffee.'

'Pils?'

'Have you turned into a prude in your old age? I need one anyway.'

She gets up and goes to the fridge, takes out two bottles and puts them on the table between us. I've never seen her drink beer except on special occasions.

'Perhaps you'll change your mind. I found them in the cellar, remnants of the Christmas party last year.'

She flips off the top with the bottle opener and drinks.

'Aren't you thirsty?' my mother asks and smiles.

'Yes, yes I am,' I reply, open my bottle and drink it straight down.

She wipes her mouth.

I take a deep breath through my nose.

'Sorry, Mother, but I'm certain that smell isn't just burnt food.'

'Don't you think I know what I'm doing?'

The snow on the bird feeder outside is beginning to disappear.

Almost all the snow that was outside the kitchen window when I came, has blown away.

'Were you ashamed of my appearance, Mother? Were you afraid we'd meet someone who knew your brother?'

She says nothing.

'You ought to go to the Genetics Unit at Ullevål Hospital,' I persist, 'as the disease originates with you.'

'How do you know it does?'

'I've been told how it works.'

'Did a doctor say that?'

I give her his name.

'He's a professor of genetics. He phoned me and asked if you were still alive, as they'd had no response from you. He told me you'd been given two appointments.'

'What have you been doing at the Genetics Unit?' she asks.

I feel a certain satisfaction at being able to conduct the conversation with a modicum of self-possession.

'Have you had a genetic test, as the doctor at Ullevål requested?' I ask.

She shakes her head.

'Uncle Frode had the same disease as me, and your father, Tor, had it. I've got it, and your experienced eyes can tell that everything points to Karoline having it. It would be useful for Karoline in the future if you took the test. It's all the more pressing now that you've got cancer.'

'Do you hate me?'

'No. Why do you ask?'

Her secrecy is different to mine, but not unlike the sort I recognize from my teenage years, when I cut myself off and refused to let anyone see in. Something that made it impossible for me to accept love—and many friendships, too.

'Do you wish I hadn't been born, Mother? Do you think it's mean of me to ask the question?'

'Could you get the three-branched candelabra out of the box on the chair next to you? That's what I've got to polish.'

I plonk the candelabra a little noisily on the table.

'Why must you go into all of this?' she says.

I feel myself grasping the table fiercely, I want to scream, I look outside, I look at her and say:

'Sunniva and I chose to have children, even though there was a considerable risk of our child inheriting the disease. It was our choice and our responsibility. There's no right or wrong in such matters, Mother. You want it all to be erased, but it's important for your grandchild to have a precise idea of how the disease has developed over the generations. It increases the chance that people in the future will find ways, using stem cells, for example, to cure the disease in Karoline. For me it's too late, but you can help her.'

'Does Karoline know that you're talking to me about all this?' my mother asks.

'Yes,' I reply.

I try to breathe calmly, swallow, make a serious effort not to look angry because that would give her an excuse to ask me to leave.

'Did Father know what your father and brother suffered from before you married?'

'No,' she says, and before I can say anything more: 'You can't put yourself in my position.'

'Of course I can't. To see a father, a brother and a son . . . and now a grandchild . . . '

I'm searching for words.

' . . . in that condition, must be difficult. Nobody can understand your torment, Mother. Nobody can deny that.'

'D'you want another beer?'

'Certainly,' I reply and take the green bottle.

'Did you speak about the disease when you and Sunniva became lovers, before you wanted to try for children?' she asks.

I let go of the table, are we really going to talk at last? Speak of our experiences? Are we going to get closer, be a bit more like other mothers and sons?

'Yes, I told her everything. I'd been silent about my big secret for far too many years. At last the words were there. Sunniva listened to me for several days.'

I assume that my mother is registering my fervour.

'She said she wanted to have my children despite all that,' I went on.

'Despite it?'

'Yes.'

'How is Karoline taking it?'

'Ask her yourself, Mother. It'll mean a lot to her. You're very important to her.'

'Have things been better for Karoline after you spoke to her?'

'Of course not. The pain is still the same,' I say, 'but Karoline has got someone she can talk to. It's the only thing we can offer.'

I look at her empty hands. Mother straightens the pile of papers in front of her and tucks in a yellowing newspaper cutting. I take it, and she makes no attempt to stop me.

The cutting is from the *Arbeiderbladet* of 14th of August 1975. The paper's name is printed on a red ground. The main story is about the new advances in medicine. I read aloud: *In a number of congenital diseases that cause serious physical and mental abnormalities, we are now able to demonstrate defects in the foetus sufficiently early to make abortion feasible.*

'Happy now?' she enquires.

Her bony hands are clutching the cup.

'What is it you were so frightened of? I can't think that Father or I would have blamed you if you'd been honest.'

She looks down at the table.

'You always said you started school in Majorstua. Isn't that right?'

'Yes,' she replies.

'I know that you started your schooling somewhere quite different, before you went there.'

We're sitting so close to each other. Between us is a mountain whose summit is impossible to see. A mountain of silence, higher and more extensive than anything else I know.

'Well, say something, Mother.'

She doesn't look up.

My class teacher at primary school, Miss Rogndokken from Valdres, said that all mothers love their children. I can remember wondering if she was right. How could Miss Rogndokken be so sure?

As if Mother can hear what I'm thinking, she says: 'I knew a mother who loved her child so much she couldn't leave it alone.'

Is she referring to the two of us?

'Surely there's something in between?' I put in.

I lay my hand on hers. She pulls her hand away. Is she cross because I've caught her off guard? Is she distraught that she's been denied the chance to take her secret to the grave with her?

I inhale.

'Mother . . . '

She's still peering down at the place mat.

' . . . I want you to know that I'm grateful for being born. You must never doubt that.'

She sighs.

'Human beings aren't nice,' she says.

I would have liked to protest, but hold my tongue.

'You don't know how horrible people are,' she continues.

'I've had some experience, Mother.'

'You don't know what it felt like to watch people snigger behind your back when you began to walk in that strange way. People are evil. I wanted children so much and kept on hoping things would work out.'

'So we've got something in common,' I remark.

'Then what happened, happened.'

I don't ask what meaning lies behind her words.

'And then it was too late,' I say.

'I must go down to the cellar. There's something I've got to show you,' she says.

'Before you go, how do you remember Tor—his appearance, his voice or something else?'

'He's gone for good.'

She places her bony, bluish-white hands on the table and pushes herself up.

'Isn't it a bit risky going down that narrow staircase in your present condition?'

'I've managed it one way or another.'

She disappears through the door without shutting it behind her, and after a while I can hear the creaking of woodwork as Mother goes slowly down the steps. I hear her moving various objects around down there, talking to herself all the while.

She's away some time. I doze.

After I'd got a girlfriend, started a family and had children, I became arrogant. I believed I could conquer anything, with a little help. Of course I searched for signs of disease in Karoline, but I'd managed to deal with life—so wouldn't a child who'd inherited the same condition manage it, too? With parents like us who could provide support and talk about the problems, wouldn't it be even easier? I ignored how ill I was becoming. I was naive enough to believe, like some religious visionary, that with a mixture of patience and willpower I would, in some vague, miraculous way, be able to surmount almost anything.

I look at the clock. It's been nearly ten minutes since she went down to the cellar. What's happened to her?

'Mother! Are you coming soon?' I shout in the direction of the open cellar door.

She makes no reply, but I can still hear her moving about down below.

I begin to go over the last time we went out together, to the National Theatre. Shuffling along I managed to get into the foyer with Mother. We ran into a couple who were mutual acquaintances. We nodded and passed each other. I halted and clutched a tall table to rest the small of my back, then turned and saw the same acquaintances, walking arm in arm, shaking their heads and talking intently. I looked around for my mother. She'd gone to the loo. I stood there supporting myself while I thought of my mother's gaze, or what I imagined was her gaze, and the couple's gaze, regarding me. The gaze that doesn't look at that which is me but to the side of it. I'm a blind spot. I am what is invisible.

I didn't want to get up next morning, I told Sunniva I'd got a migraine. What I wanted most of all was to turn into a heavy stone.

I realize that Mother doesn't want to talk. That's her right. Just as it's my right to imagine how her story may have evolved.

At the time when the disease had begun to affect Tor's ability to move about, there were no doctors capable of providing the neurological explanation available to us now.

It must have come as an incomprehensible shock that Grandfather found it harder and harder to walk. The fact that he took a drink now and again made it only natural for Grandma to blame alcohol when she had to explain what was wrong with her husband. Alcohol is tangible. When you have no diagnosis the situation is difficult to explain. What an agony it must have been to realize that your son had the same condition as his father. Frode's state visibly worsened. Could they have rationalized his uncouth movements as a mild variant of Spanish flu? It arrived in Norway and spread during 1918 and 1919, the year he was born. The tendon complications of Spanish flu often appeared several years later. I don't know. It's possible alcohol was blamed to avoid naming a disease associated with even greater shame: syphilis. Syphilis is often described as 'the great imitator' in medical history. A number of symptoms of the disease, which today would be listed as characteristic of Parkinson's disease or the disease I've got, were then seen as signs of late-stage syphilis. In spite of everything, alcohol had less stigma attached to it than syphilis. The disease was associated with dissolute sexual behaviour.

I wheel my chair out to the loo which is adjacent to the kitchen. I glance at my watch. I can hear something falling over in the kitchen. She's obviously returned from the cellar.

'What are you doing?' I yell.

She makes no answer.

I return to the kitchen and push open the door with my foot. There is smoke in the room and water on the floor, together with some scorched paper. She's opened the window.

Through the glass pane in the oven door I can see a pile of burnt papers and photos. Mother is standing next to the cooker with a blue plastic bucket.

'Well, that's done,' she says

She looks satisfied.

I look at the floor.

'Is the fire out?'

She nods.

'Don't worry about that. I'll clean up afterwards.'

She closes the window.

I lean forward, then to the side, looking at the glass panel in the oven door.

'What is it?' she asks.

'Be careful when you burn the rest,' I tell her.

The taxi driver turns up on time. He hauls the wheelchair backwards over the doorstep and out.

Even though it will soon be Christmas, snow hasn't settled on the ground.

'No need to bring flowers next time you come,' Mother says and waves.

I fix my gaze on the birch tree in front of the car. It's quivering. Snow falls on the leaves beneath the tree.

After the driver has helped me into the back seat, I try to recall a name the consultant geneticist at Ullevål Hospital mentioned during my follow-up at the end of August. I'd asked which physician or medic had made the greatest impression on him. I remember that it was some American with a German name. It annoys me that I didn't write it down. I get out my mobile. Was it Møller? The name comes up almost immediately.

Herman Joseph Muller.

I scroll through an article about the eugenicists who maintained that one race was superior to another. They were in the dock at Nuremburg after the Second World War. Further down I read about *Man's Future Birthright* published in 1956, in which Muller says that although it's a human right to have one's defects treated with all the means at society's disposal, no one should have the right to pass on so many genetic, or partially genetic, defects, as to increase the load on society.

The article says that Muller was neither a Nazi nor a eugenicist. He was an advocate of 'germinal choice'. He spoke out on behalf of humanity. He was awarded the Nobel Prize for his pioneering work in physiology and medicine. The award was made in 1946, just when the Nuremburg trials were starting. That same year he was voted humanist of the year in the USA. I was born eight years later. Mother, Grandma, Muller and I are all a part of the spirit of that age.

Google also brings up an article by a Swedish doctor who'd attended a congress where public health legacy problems were discussed.

In 2015, Professor Aris Antsaklis, president of the World Association of Perinatal Medicine, had opened the organization's international congress in Madrid. Perinatal medicine covers the period from twenty-two weeks' gestation to seven days after birth. Antsaklis used his address to talk about the possibilities of detecting foetal abnormality using modern technology. He raised no ethical questions or concerns. The medical and pharmaceutical industries were well represented at the congress. Perinatal physicians have taken on the role played by public health legacy campaigners in the 1930s.

The Swedish doctor informed us that it is now possible to buy genetic test kits from pharmacies that can indicate a tendency to obesity, a risk of blood clots, lactose intolerance or athletic prowess. We can study the ACTN3 gene and find out whether our offspring will have muscles suited to explosive activity or endurance. The new eugenics, according to this doctor, is neither brutal nor cruel. It is human, because doctors now use new technology which, in the long run, will be good for mankind. He refers to a German colleague who took the floor to say that he disagreed with the majority of the congress. 'The very individuals you all want to root out,' he said, 'individuals with defects, could, if they were allowed to live, contribute to the human race.'

I switch off my mobile phone. The last light particles dissipate in the darkness of the taxi. Street lighting has been switched on outside.

In front of me, the driver steers. I can hear the diesel engine's even hum. We only stop for red lights, and we say nothing.

Sparks fly every time the pedals strike the chain-casing. The light beam flickers restlessly ahead of me, as I pedal with all my strength.

The dynamo whines causing the dented lamp's solitary bulb to emit particles of light. The darkness envelops the shaft of light, the bike and me. The maple trees on the right are invisible.

I can feel my ankle against the parquet.

My right ear is pointing towards the floor.

One day the earth will have had enough.

The stars will be sluiced down the heavenly sewer.

The earth will shake itself the way a dog shakes off water.

We will be hurled into space.

I confess: I'd like to be saved.

I blink and feel my eyelashes touch my cheeks just under my eye sockets.

My nose probably looks much the same as the last time I saw it in the mirror.

Then it was straight.

I'm glad it was operated on by a skilful surgeon.

My nose and ankles have suffered complicated fractures, but today, viewed in isolation, they have an appearance nobody would find remarkable.

My ankles are symmetrical and look as if they're fit for walking.

We drive down Bogstadveien, where Eline once saw me walking with Grandma. Perhaps she followed us as we turned and went into Pettersen the butterman's, where Grandma bought thickly sliced Swiss cheese. The slices were wrapped in white paper with a thin, transparent foil between each slice.

Now people are hurrying in and out of the shops. The taxi stops several times because of traffic heading towards the city centre. I ponder mother's motives for silence. Is it malicious at all? It could be contempt, not to mention fear, of being different, of weakness, but most of all I sense an attitude that alternates between anger and sorrow. But I still don't understand why.

Then, as now, the state and society want as little of my sort as possible. There's no point in romanticizing my life.

Mother and Grandma could have made a lifelong pact in the belief that it would be best for me not to know the truth. I won't get any more answers and I'll just have to live with that. I must accept it, relax, breathe in, look out, and think about something else.

The driver, who's driven me countless times, comments on the hysterical Christmas shopping we witness through the car windows. He's noticed that I'm quieter than usual.

We usually talk about sport at this time of year, ski sport, preferably jumping. Several times I've remarked to myself that he does just the right amount of talking.

There's another red light. Through the window I can hear the ticking noise that tells the blind it's safe for pedestrians to cross.

I'm about to pull my scarf tighter when I discover that I've forgotten it. The driver sees me in his mirror and asks what the matter is.

'Nothing,' I say.

In the back of the taxi I think of what my mother might have told her brother when she stopped going to Vaterland School and began at Majorstuen. Nine-year-olds understand more than we think. I still remember how surprised I was at Karoline's mature and philosophical questions about what it was like to inhabit my body. Mother might have had some clue, but it's unlikely she knew everything. She never blamed Grandma or spoke disparagingly about her.

For my own part, I sense that Mother was the more controlling of the two. Grandma listened and never contradicted her daughter when my father or I were present. But I don't *know*.

I must resign myself to the fact that no archive or library will ever reveal what they said in private.

I got out my phone and read through Grandfather's love letter to Grandma again. The letter contains not a single reproach, quite the contrary. It gives the impression that he loves her, they don't appear to have disagreed about anything at all. There's nothing in this letter, or anywhere else, that indicates he'd had a problem with alcohol. Until Mother showed me the letter, I was indignant at the way Grandma had deserted her sick husband.

The letter lessened my conviction. What if he'd asked her to leave him on his own in Elvegata and make the best of the situation? If a family goes hiking in the mountains and the father breaks his leg just as they're being overtaken by a terrific storm, wouldn't any father with a sense of honour tell his wife to leave him and save herself and the children? Neither can I dismiss the idea that Tor might have reckoned Grandma had a better chance of finding another husband and provider if she had only one child with her, a good-looking girl, and not two. He might have had a hand in these choices, too. Or was he forced into it? It's an uncertainty I have to live with. Wasn't it understandable that Grandma didn't want to introduce me to the sufferings she'd undergone, and the difficult choices she'd faced? Trying to expunge Tor's existence might have been painful and distasteful while he lived but it might also have got worse over the years and harder for Grandma and Mother to explain to others. Nevertheless they probably hoped that time and oblivion would come to their aid.

The day before Sunniva left for Svalbard, I had an e-mail from the City Archives. The sender was Christine Wood. 'Hope you're well. I thought this might be of interest. C.W.'

That was all. Below the greeting was a link to the National Library's online archive. I clicked on the link. The screen was filled with a christening photograph. The picture might have been the subject of a Carl Larsen painting or a composition by one of the Skagen artists: Man holding a baby. In front of him stands a blonde boy with large, gentle eyes wearing a sailor suit. The boy might have been me. At the age I was when I stood on the tortoise in Addis Ababa. Beneath the photo is the legend: *Christening at Nesoddtangen, 29th of August 1925* and the three names.

The boy is my Uncle Frode. He's leaning back against his father. His father's got a crew cut and is gazing happily at the fine little lass he's holding in his arms. He looks as if he's wearing a linen shirt. His trousers are light coloured. In the background, to the left, there's a white bathing hut with a ladder leading down into the water. The man in the picture is Grandfather. He's carrying Mother at her christening.

I search for creases in Tor's face, look at the way he holds himself, trying to detect signs of the disease. He's in his late thirties and has adopted a pose I often used at that age to make it harder to see that my shoulders, stomach and mouth were an unusual shape. My grandfather is facing the waves. Behind him, behind the flat rocks of the shore, is a tall spruce. If the photo were in colour, it would have been green. I don't know if Grandma took the picture. Perhaps she was standing right in front of her husband, in a white dress, with her straw hat at a jaunty angle as he caught the scent of roses. It's possible he can't see the sunset, but perhaps he glimpses his own shadow and feels a trembling in his soul as he holds his daughter. He could, if he turned his head to the side and raised his eyes, have made out the blue wooded hills on the far side of the fjord.

I get out my phone and find Google maps. I've got the address of the house by the fjord where they lived. As if I'm controlling a camera on a drone, I focus in on Oslo City Hall, then down to Honnørbrygga, out into the fjord, to the nearest peninsula. I find the place almost immediately. A detached house still stands there. Though similar, it's been remodelled. The florid 'dragon style' has been retained, but there's a modern extension, and the house has been painted dark blue. I shift the focus a little to the right. There is the white bathing hut, as before. I stare at the bathing ladder which angles down towards the mirror-like ice. I imagine cod twisting back and forth beneath the ice, their eyes glittering between the kelp and seaweed.

When I was a boy, a youth and a young man, my identity was fixed by the person I saw in the mirror. After I was diagnosed, I spent longer and longer scrutinizing the tiny deformities in my face. Otherness became my new identity. Once I'd passed forty, I looked in the mirror less.

Now, as often as I can, preferably every day, I try to see Oslofjord. The play between the sky, the water and the hills, in all seasons, is what I interpret to be me. Until I saw the photograph on the screen in front of me. It was then I found the piece of my narrative that I lacked.

I've made a copy of the picture of Grandfather with his children. It's the final part of my own history. The picture hangs above my writing table, fixed with a couple of drawing pins. When I gaze at my uncle and grandfather, it's myself I see.

It's night, and I lie waiting for the sun to strike my part of the Earth.

Snow is sifting down from the sky.

Colours disappear.

Snow crystals evoke a black-and-white photo.

Now the ski-jumping slopes can be made ready.

My feet are cold.

I prop myself on my right elbow.

I see the reflection from a street light.

I repeat several of the exchanges between my mother and me.

My voice sounds alien, as when I hear it on a recording.

It's complex, nuanced.

It has innumerable shades and dimensions.

It's the garb of my unruly thoughts but I do not recognize it.

It's the voice inside my head that's mine.

I turn my head.

I look at the ceiling.

The snow has stopped falling outside.

I roll over on to my back.

Jan Mayen lies beneath the right half of my torso.

My shoulder blade is pressing down on Barentsburg.

My heart is thudding obdurately in my ribcage.

My brain is lying curled in my cranium, like a dog in front of the fireplace.

I raise my hands, my loyal servers, my flowers, birds, claws, pincers.

There's a pricking at my temples.

Here within the darkness my body becomes indistinct, near to the mineral kingdom.

The moon regards me through the curtain and does nothing.

Voices, words, sentences.

Clearer, close.

I can hear someone unlocking the door.

A man's deep voice says: *'It's easy enough to forget a key.'*

It's the caretaker speaking.

'Did you see the northern lights a few days ago?' he continues. 'The tail was iridescent green and it was going like a whip.'

'He must be here,' says a lighter voice. 'He can't go out on his own. I can't understand why he doesn't answer his phone.'

I recognize the voice.

I shout: 'I've got something to tell you, Karoline!'

I shout louder.

THE TWENTY-THIRD OF DECEMBER

Yesterday evening Sunniva came home from Svalbard. First thing this morning she helped me into the electric wheelchair I use outside. It's got four-wheel drive and is controlled from a panel attached to the right armrest. The battery lasts for three hours. It's my electric horse. It's been two years since my occupational therapist talked me into trying one. I had hesitated. 'Feeling self-conscious?' she asked. 'Wouldn't it be rather nice to get out into the country again with Sunniva, or drive along next to her while she's jogging?'

Now I look forward to every jaunt outdoors.

I needed to visit my optician for help with tightening the hinges of my glasses, and set out on my journey to the shopping centre at Lambertseter. I was packed in a sleeping bag and wore an insulated jacket, scarf, gloves and a lined leather pilot hat with ear flaps. Inside the sleeping bag my feet were encased in short boots with woollen soles.

The roads were icy. Drivers were being cautious. Pedestrians, whether they had crampons or not, walked gingerly. Even though I was well wrapped up, the cold began to seep into my feet. I switched on my two small headlights so that I'd be easier to see. People who didn't know me, gave me a wide berth, their mouths agape. Children under school age sent me envious stares and tugged at their grown-ups' coats and jackets. 'Mum, Dad, I want one of those for Christmas!' I heard as I put on speed to demonstrate my pace and power.

The usual automatic door of the shopping centre had jammed. I had to drive round the large building to a rear exit that was locked and wait for someone to come out. At last a smiling elderly woman using a rollator with two carrier bags attached came along. She tried to manoeuvre through the wide door. At the risk of slipping on the icy stone slabs herself, she held the door open for me. I could see it was an effort for her. I thanked her as I went in. As soon as she was out of sight, I put my foot down.

My journey continued down a long corridor that turned sharply to the left. Moments later I found myself among a troop of Christmas elves, well up in years, some with and some without, accordions. They quickly moved aside. A large group of onlookers appeared in front of me. Some of them gawped at me open-mouthed. I rolled on, a little more slowly, and halted between the display windows at the optician's. I removed my cap and gloves, while the elves I'd just met launched into 'Away in a Manger'.

With my glasses adjusted and the lenses polished, I drove past the off-licence and the bookshop. An interior design outlet brought me to an abrupt halt. I put on my glasses to make certain my eyes weren't deceiving me. From the ceiling of the store, a bunch of roses was dangling upside down. The stems were tied with a thread. The petals looked as if they'd been made of deep red, crinkly paper. A remnant of the scarlet hue clung to their wrinkled edges. Just then, as I was contemplating the things we use as decoration, an incident flashed up in my memory.

The light is at first fluorescent, then light yellow and then deep yellow, granular, almost orange. Mother and Grandma are in Grandma's living room. I can see a portion of them through the door which stands ajar at the end of the corridor. The door was open when my mother asked me to fetch Grandma a large glass of water, and I went to the kitchen. I am fourteen and it's the school holidays. It's hot, high summer. I hear raised voices. I stop dead, a little water slops over the rim of the glass and down on to the mat. I see my mother's face in profile. She stands over Grandma who's pushing at her and turning her head away. I take a step forward, they hear me and go quiet. When I open the door wide, they're each sitting in their own chairs as if nothing has happened. Grandma thanks me and Mother smiles.

I drew a deep breath, put on my headgear with its large ear flaps and whizzed out of the centre like a cocker spaniel that's slipped its leash.

Outside the mist had thinned beneath the grey clouds. I made for Brannfjell and took the path to the summit to look at the fjord, with Gressholmen directly opposite.

Sixteen years had passed since I'd last stood on my own two legs here by the cairn and admired the view. At that time Karoline had just started school and Sunniva had helped me up the half mile of path. I wasn't the least bit tired, I smiled, I could raise my head and look over the water. I took in clouds, sky, passing planes, and didn't have to watch my feet all the time in case I tripped.

The mobility aid provided some of the same joy I'd had in the days when I could swim through the water in whatever direction I liked, doing the crawl, the breast- or the backstroke.

I drove down Ekebergåsen and past the Ekeberg restaurant just as the Ljabru tram ground its metal wheels hard into the rails. The two cars were about to grapple with the steepest gradient after passing the Maritime College. The lights inside the cars made them look like a couple of aquaria rising towards the evening sky.

I looked past the lofty pine trees until my eyes came to rest on the grey and snow-decked islands in the fjord. I steered down Karlsborgveien to take in the fjord and the spot where Sunniva and I used to bathe.

I crossed Mosseveien to get as close to the grey, wintery waves as possible. I switched off the motor at the far end of a concrete breakwater. The foam formed strips which came forging in, one after the other, under the surface. They became more defined, with a small white edge, as they smashed themselves against the rocks. They ran out again. One wave followed the next. They grew, rose and sharpened, before they fell, and the foam was hurled back.